OUR TIME

Adam Ciancio is a writer and director with a focus on film and television. The idea for *Our Time* originated over twelve years ago, when his sister had a dream about people with clocks embedded in their chests, counting down the moments until their deaths. This intriguing concept sparked Adam's decade-long journey to develop the screenplay. By 2020, an A-list actor became involved, taking on the lead role and also serving as producer. Just as the project gained momentum and casting for the female lead was underway, the COVID-19 pandemic halted production. Despite this setback, a recurring comment throughout the project's development stuck with Adam: "It feels like we're adapting a novel that hasn't been written yet." Inspired by this, Adam decided to transform Our Time from a screenplay into a novel.

Adam Ciancio

OUR TIME

To my family, whose unwavering love and support have been my foundation, guiding me through every chapter of life with strength and grace.

To my friends, the chosen family who fill my world with laughter, understanding, and the kind of connection that transcends time and distance.

And to the new relationships—those uncharted bonds that bring fresh perspectives and joy, reminding me that there is always room for growth and new beginnings.

This story is possible because of you, and the countless ways you make life richer and more meaningful.

PROLOGUE

The talk show TV set was designed in those non-offensive, neutral prime-time colors. Lacey Young sat behind a desk to the right of the stage, with a long couch in front for her guests. A faux silhouette of the city skyline stretched behind her— the one that most talk shows used to give the impression their program was happening in the hustle and bustle of some mega metropolis instead of some soundstage in Los Angeles. Next to her sat a man.

Montgomery Dunn.

He was in his mid twenties; handsome but nerdy. He was dressed in a suit and tie, and didn't give off any celebrity vibe. He was a little more uptight—being on camera wasn't his first job, it wasn't even his second job. Montgomery wasn't an actor, musician or athlete;. He was a scientist and, right at this moment, quite possibly, the most important person in the world, if not the history of the world.

"So we're back with Doctor Montgomery Dunn."

The audience cheered, prompting Montgomery to stop staring at the faux background and give the unsurest of smiles to Lacey,

"So, you are the man who discovered Nox Anima?" Lacey wasn't used to interviewing a scientist so she had affected a more serious tone and seating position to match the gravity of what they were about to discuss.

Montgomery smiled and nodded. "Yeah, that's… correct."

She leaned in. "So tell us a little more about this mutation and its sudden spread across the globe?" She watched Montgomery breathe in; it wasn't an easy thing to convey what this mutation was without alarming people but she wanted to make sure her audience were equipped with all the answers. Yet even with all the answers, there was nothing the average citizen could really do about it. The mutation had become such a force in such little time that it had upended the basic ways in which people in society had engaged with one another. A very clear narrative rose amongst the general population. Either you had Nox Anima or you didn't and it was terrifying how quickly it was beginning to divide the population.

Finally he spoke, "Well, the mutation is termed Nox Anima, which is Latin for Without Life. It is a genetic mutation that appears to occur during the first trimester of pregnancy but doesn't make itself present until birth. We don't know where it has come from or how it came about, but as we've all noticed, it has become a global problem almost instantly."

Lacey chimed in again. "And how does it work?"

Montgomery thought for a moment. "So basically what Nox Anima does is release toxins that convince your organs to fail at a predetermined year. Usually between the ages of twenty-seven and thirty."

"So like a timebomb?"

"Yeah, if you want to put it that way, but we have to be careful not to brand anyone with it as different from those without it. It's random selection and our entire focus right now as a society should solely be on finding a cure."

Lacey nodded and took the lead. "So what *do you* have in a possible cure?"

He didn't want to peddle false hope but he did want people to know his team was working day and night to fix this phenomenon. "We've got something. It's shown incredible promise in reversing the mutation once the child is born and I'm hoping it will be ready in the next eighteen to twenty-four months."

The camera held on Montgomery.

"Well you're doing incredible work and the world thanks you. Can we give Montgomery a hand?"

The audience erupted in a louder than usual cheer offered to a run of the mil actor or singer—a sound Montgomery wasn't used to, but quickly grew on him…

CHAPTER 1
THIRTY YEARS LATER

The morning light gleaned through the window and touched Josephine Dunn in the face. It wasn't harsh. Nothing in her world was harsh. She remained asleep for a few minutes before she truly woke up and felt the sun's warmth.

Rubbing the sleep from her eyes, she sat up on her elbows and looked around her dorm room. It was bizarrely empty—no desk, no TV, no books. She only had posters and a bed with clothes strewn around it in random piles. Early chatter, birds and bells—the noises of the university campus—were starting to filter through.

Josephine was twenty-three and a student studying social science with a major in sociology.

As the sleep faded, her eyes intensified. There was a focus to her gaze that gave you the impression that you couldn't get anything past her. When you talked, she listened and, most importantly, remembered. Her hair was dark, thick and somewhat wavy, and she wore it in a ponytail most of the time. She had more important issues to deal with than how to tame her chunky hair.

The energy she carried made her magnetic; you just

knew she was going to make a difference, she definitely did. The drive and self-belief had been drummed into her from an early age by her father and had stuck with her, even after he lost his own aspirations.

Reaching behind her ear, she pushed a small purple button. A pleasant chime accompanied a semi-transparent projection that beamed out from her eye and hovered in front of her. The screen was not unlike a desktop computer home screen, her wallpaper showed her at a university rally. This was her OurCloud, something that every student on campus was in possession of. She didn't speak but the voice in her head prompted the commands.

"*Alarm off*" —An alarm set for seven switched off.

"*Log in*" —A password box popped up.

"*BEVERLINE*" —The text was entered in discreet dots and gave Josephine access to her account. Her profile page loaded instantly.

"*Check schedule*" —A calendar popped up populated with different colored squares, most of them classes, some of them catch ups, and a few of them marked *personal time*.

"*Set reminder, visit dad in six hours*" —the reminder was set and then faded out.

A message popped up from Elizabeth.

"*Open message*" —The message was a combination of text and emojis.

"Read message" —A bubbly, female voice filled her head.

> "Don't forget, I set that date up for you. Don't stand him up like the last one; women are throwing themselves at him…"

"Stop reading" —Josephine cut off the message before it had time to finish. She pressed the button behind her ear and the projection screen retreated back into her eye. She clapped her hands and spoke out loud for the first time. "Time to be the difference."

On the other side of town stood Kit Dent. He was twenty-seven, rough around the edges, and looked like someone who could handle himself in a fight. Not in a way that would have him looking for trouble. It was more a sturdiness, a worldliness—he'd seen a lot in his twenty-seven years as a Rat, so little scared him, and even less surprised him. He was fully comfortable in his body. He'd thrashed it around for almost three decades now and knew his time was coming to an end, so that air of cool that comes with not giving a damn was undeniable. It was what made him sexy.

He wore a t-shirt with his sleeves rolled up that exposed a small collection of random tattoos. His dirty, ripped jeans somehow looked like they were never meant to be clean and his boots were scuffed but still maintained that feel of old world craftsmanship. In fact the only thing that looked new was his watch—heavy, silver, and hosting a sapphire green clock face. It was his look and he totally owned it.

His gaze was fixed on a heavily tattooed dead body lying on the floor. A tarp was being pulled over it by thick men wearing uniforms that were an imposing mesh of police and paramedic. As the tarp rose up the torso, Kit's eyes drifted to the corpse's shoulder. That unmistakable blue sub dermal ring glowed from under the dead man's now greying skin. Inside it was a dark red cross that had the appearance and texture of an indicator you'd see in a pregnancy test. The red cross was produced by Nox Anima's toxins, the only thing science was able to achieve in the last twenty-five years. The blue ring was a stamp made mandatory by the government.

Kit rubbed his own shoulder.

"Hey you listening?"

The voice was gruff, old and tired. Kit turned to face Detective Flint, a man in his mid-fifties who dealt only in absolutes. A man whose entire life was dedicated to stopping the spread of NOX ANIMA, the mysterious mutation that rocked the world thirty years ago. At this point of his career, he had built a reputation as someone who would rather seek the easy answers instead of the right ones.

A photo frame was shoved into Kit's chest, he locked eyes with the lingering Detective who stood there waiting for Kit to give him the answers he needed—the easy ones… "You seen her?"

Kit studied the photo lazily. Both knew the answer was going to be "No," but Kit played along for the sake of keeping the peace. In the frame was a couple. The man was covered head to toe in tattoos, with the physique of someone who was, at minimum, an avid cross-fitter. Ultimately, he looked like someone who would hang out with Kit. His attire screamed punk rap, with a dash of street skate, torn jeans, gaudy jewelry, backwards hat. It all looked trashy but still expensive. His entire personality on display in his ink, muscles and clothing—not to mention a dazzling watch that finished off the look. The timepiece was the badge of honor that every Nox Anima sufferer wore in a bid to make them feel like a collective force. Not only that, it was the thing they used to tell the time—the one thing they had little of. The watch was, in effect, a modern day coat of arms of their people, the RATS.

The man in the photo had his hand lovingly resting on the belly of a woman, heavily pregnant, definitely in her third trimester. If he was the epitome of cutting edge street culture, her look could only be described as Scandinavian chic—her personality tightly held within the carefully layered colors, none of them bold, all of them worked in perfect harmony, a range of blues and greys and browns, all oversized and all giving the perception that she never once thought about what she was going to wear. She woke up this way and the clothes just fell in that sequence, like a haute couture Tetris.

They looked happy, but their joy betrayed what they really felt: Fear. You could see it in their eyes. They knew this was not forever. They were making the most of the moment and wanted to make sure it was freeze locked forever so they could always go back and visit it.

Detective Flint leaned into Kit's line of sight. "So?"

A chewing sound broke the stand off. Jim Kane. Kit's best friend since childhood. Jim waltzed in and leaned over, taking a non committal glance at the photo frame. If Kit carried himself with a resigned cool, Jim was a make-every-second-count type of guy. There was an energy to him that bordered on aggressive but that was if you didn't know him. To his friends, he was loyal.

His sinewy arms popped out of his sleeveless hoodie, the edges frayed, because he ripped the sleeves off himself. His arms were covered in designer ink only stopping at the edge of his shoulder to make way for his own blue glowing sub dermal ring, his *stamp* A branding he wore as a *fuck you* to the rest of the world. Whilst Kit found it more comfortable to cover his up, Jim wanted anyone and everyone to see it—the more uncomfortable you felt around him, the better. He wasn't here to make your life easier, especially if you didn't have Nox Anima.

Jim looked up at the detective and, still chewing on his hoodie cord, offered a slobbery "Nope."

"What was that?" Detective Flint fired back. He knew what the answer was. What he was looking for was some respect, something he had been fighting for more and more as he got older. Back in his early days, he was able to relate to these kids. But now that he was middle aged, he was just another asshole cop who spent his days arresting those with Nox Anima and it had made him an enemy to the rest of the community.

Jim spat out his hoodie cord. "No."

Detective Flint gritted his teeth and snatched the frame from Kit's hands before muttering loud enough so the two of them could hear it. A phrase he knew would send Jim into a spin, "Fucking Rats."

"What did you call us?" Jim threw his body, forward invading the detective's space.

Kit held Jim firmly in place.

The detective leaned in. The two were now only inches away. Both men lived for these moments, especially the detective. They were the only ones that made him feel alive, highlights peppered throughout mountains of police paperwork.

"You heard me. What are you going to do?" He shot Jim a smug smile.

"Forget him," Kit said.

The derogatory term was something similar to the word WOP, or Gook or the N word. A term taken back by those with Nox Anima ten years prior in a bid to stop those without it from weaponizing it against them. Yet even with taking ownership of this word, it didn't mean it still couldn't be used. It just depended on how much venom that person added when they were saying it.

The term RAT stood for Racing Against Time. Not only poking fun at Nox Anima sufferers' lack of time on the planet but also the hurried way in which they rushed through life.

Kit gradually pulled Jim away, who refused to break eye contact with the detective, who was already out the door.

"Come on, we got work to do." Kit walked back to their room.

CHAPTER 2
WHAT'S THAT NOISE?

Moments later, Jim and Kit began clearing items from the bedroom. Sounds from other rooms could be heard. Their job was simple: Clear every last bit of this dead Rat's life and put it into boxes so it could be re-sold in the cash economy that only Rats had access to.

The difference between how the boys respected the memories of this man were clear. Kit carefully placed each item in a box, whilst Jim swiped the belongings with his forearm like a snow plow, pausing only to pocket the poor dead guy's gaudy gold watch.

Kit wasn't averse to stealing a dead Rat's belongings but it was never anything more than random collectibles. In this case, he halted on a small toy dinosaur. It felt out of context with the rest of the stuff in the room, and made Kit think about this guy, like deep down, even at the age of twenty-eight, he was really just a little boy terrified of the harshness of life and forbidden love. The toy was perfect for Kit's bowl of trinkets. It was his way of respecting the memories of these people. Otherwise, their items would just recirculate forever and ever, from one nameless Rat to the next.

The clinking of coat hangers coming off metal only meant one thing. Clothes were being racked off and thrown onto the bed. The entire closet was stacked with ripped designer jeans, loud jackets, rare sneakers, expensive belts and t-shirts emblazoned with big luxury brand logos. Kit racked off the last of the jackets when he heard a muffled noise. He didn't make much of it until he heard it again. Turning around, he held his breath, hoping not to hear it one more time. There it was again, but this time he was able to decipher it. It was a gurgling sound, not like a drain. This was something different, something human. He slowly crept towards the back of the closet, pressed his ear against the timber, and waited.

There it was again. What the hell was it? He pulled back and studied what he knew now was a false wall. He pressed on each corner and felt the joints buckling. He jiggled the panel to one side as he dug his fingers underneath it and *Thunk* the panel lifted off, making the sounds behind it clear as day. What lay behind it was shocking.

There, huddled in a corner, trembling and unable to make eye contact, was a woman holding a grizzling baby, not just a woman but *the woman* from the photo.

Gone was the tasteful Scandinavian clothing, poise and joy, replaced by a petrified mother cradling her newborn. The light from the apartment bedroom blinded her tear stained face like God's flashlight.

Kit stepped back, speechless, the silent time between them felt like an eternity until she painfully sputtered out - "Please don't let them take my baby."

Kit, frozen in shock, struggled with the scenario. He closed the closet doors carefully, muffling the sound of both the woman's whimpering and the baby's grizzling. He stood there not knowing what to do. His mind was blank; only the image of what he had just seen remained.

Jim was behind him pulling down the wall mounted flat screen off its hinges. When he noticed the silence, he turned around to find Kit standing there, staring at the closet. "Kit, what the fuck man?"

Kit didn't respond.

Jim returned the TV to its wall brackets and walked over to face him. "Kit?"

Kit's eyes did all the talking and motioned him silently to the closet.

Jim looked at Kit again, wondering if his best friend was having a mild stroke. He sensed he needed to look inside that closet so he inched closer, inspected the two doors of the closet, and pressed his ear against it. There it was, the whimpering and the crying. He whipped back at Kit, his face saying it all: "WTF?"

Deftly, he reached out and pulled the doors revealing the mum once again and her child.

She looked up at Jim this time, still crying, still shaking, hoping these two Rats wouldn't turn her in, hoping the fact they were of her lover's people they would take mercy on her.

Jim backed up to Kit and whispered, "Dude we gotta tell the boss."

Kit shot back. "There is a fucking baby in there!"

The two of them communicated in low and sharp tones, both wanting to make their point but not make a scene.

Jim gritted his teeth. "What do you think would have happened if she found one of us in there?" He let it sink in knowing there was no way Kit could counter it. "Yeah that's right. She would do us in. I'm not losing my job because a "Clean Skin" fucked a Rat. Be smart, think about your Nan."

Clean Skin was the term used by the Rats when talking about those without Nox Anima. Nobody knew where the term came from but it alluded to the fact they weren't stamped on the shoulder like the rest of them; hence, their shoulders were clean.

Jim was right but Kit couldn't help be broken by the circle of life about to be ripped apart. He lowered his head, and Jim needed no more acknowledgment that they were in agreement.

As he went to locate the boss, he left Kit there to revel in the deathly silence between him and this mother and child. Kit knew that she knew what was about to happen and he could barely lift his head to look at her anymore. He wondered if this was his fault. Or was he just obeying the law?

The rules were black and white. A Clean Skin couldn't engage in a relationship with a Rat for fear of spreading Nox Anima amongst the Clean Skin community. But admittedly, it was more that a Rat couldn't engage with a Clean Skin, an insidious law by the government to let Rats slowly breed themselves out of existence. The rule was black and white but love between a Rat and Clean Skin always sat deeply in the grey.

Moments later, the apartment became a cacophony of struggles and screaming. Both Kit and Jim hung outside the room. They heard the resistance as the woman battled the police and burly removal guys.

"No! Give me back my baby."

Her crying was so desperate and piercing that it had set her baby off, whose cry had reached that sustained baby wail that would make any heart sink.

As her body was ragdolled out of the bedroom and her baby carried out by one of the low level police officers, Detective Flint hung by, waiting to read her the charges. Years ago, he lived for this stuff, but the longer he served, the harder it became. Instead of becoming hardened to this type of scene, he found the only way to get through it was to read it out as if reading the instructions from a whitegoods manual. "Alexandria Frey, you are under arrest for engaging in a sexual relationship with a Rat and breaking the reproduction rule, therefore further contributing to the spread of Nox Anima amongst the general population. Your baby being a carrier of the mutation will now be treated as a ward of the state."

With that final line, she broke down, "NO!" Her body whipped and jerked. It was her one last attempt to free herself, but her prototypical, waify, Clean Skin body was useless compared to the day in day out muscle of the police.

Detective Flint, with a cold detachment, looked at the burly men trying to handle her. "Take her away."

Kit and Jim remained glued with their backs to the wall. Jim watched the whole scenario play out with a level of pitied curiosity whilst Kit couldn't bare to lift up his head.

As Detective Flint passed the guys, he offered them a knowing nod as if to say: *You did the right thing gentlemen.*

The screams and wails carried on down the hall, leaving everyone, including the other removalists, to remain still for a moment, lamenting in the scene they just witnessed.

"All right... shows over!" The voice boomed from Boss Man as he surged down the hallway. A bear of a unit, he clapped his hands together and they made the sound of a car backfiring. "We got five more houses today… back to work!"

Scenes like this were not an excuse for the outfit to not meet their daily clearance quota. This was their world, and they did not have the time to give a fuck about that woman or that baby. Just another dumb Clean Skin who flew too close to the sun.

Jim left Kit there on the wall and went back into the room. Kit could still hear the shrill of that woman's voice ringing in his ears. He wasn't completely aware, but this felt like a moment, a pivotal point, something that inverted how he perceived his place in the world. But why now?

He had seen scenes like this before. It was just part of being a Rat. But maybe, knowing that at any moment he could wake up, walk to the mirror and find that unmistakable red cross on his shoulder, made him think that he should make these final moments count. That was, make it count in a way that wasn't how his Rat friends made these moments count. But how would he do that, and what would that involve?

CHAPTER 3
ARE YOU READY FOR A FIGHT?

Josephine sat dead in the middle of a crammed lecture theatre, unfocused on what was being relayed to her by Professor Braithewaite. Instead she was scribbling some notes on a ripped up piece of paper. A speech; words were crossed out, replaced with new ones, others were jotted in short hand on the side. Arrows directed the flow of the speech one way only to flip it back on itself midway through and start again.

One particular formula stood out in her scratchings, it read CLEAN SKINS : TIME > MONEY whilst RATS: MONEY > TIME.

The way she was marking and re-marking made it clear there was an urgency to this work. On a wider scale, amongst her university class mates, Josephine's dark complexion created a stark contrast to her Scandinavian style. In a theatre full of kids dressed like they were walking the runway in a fashion show in Copenhagen, Josephine stood out, the colors complementing her better. Or maybe the eye was just drawn towards her intensity.

Professor Braithewaite paced the front. His beard, jacket, glasses and shoes all screamed a life of learning and education. He was a little soft around the mid section. You couldn't imagine this man existing in the world Kit and Jim lived in; yet here he was, theorizing about the social ramifications of Nox Anima today.

Behind him, large letters were scribbled on the whiteboard. They read: *NOX ANIMA and its effects on the social construct.* He was midway through a rambling monologue but his manner was enough to keep most of the students interested.

He cleared his throat and prepared himself to see how well his students were listening and how engaging an educator he was. "Hence the stamping act being introduced. What I want to know is, what were the implications of forcing those with Nox Anima to be stamped?"

In one corner of the lecture theatre, a luminescent screen popped. It was someone's OurCloud.

The Professor stopped his ramble and his walk, the light catching his eye. Without missing a beat or even looking at the offending student, he pointed and curtly. "Clouds down!"

The screen immediately sucked back into the eye of the student.

He held still just long enough to make sure he and the rest of the class knew that he didn't tolerate clouds in his class. He took a breath and softened his expression again. "So my question is, was it ethical? Was it even legal? Should we have done something about it? Could we have done something about it?" He waited and looked around, hoping that his students would do him proud. "Anyone?" He threw up his hands, hoping to welcome an opinion, any opinion.

A few hands tentatively rose up. He ignored them all; instead, he pointed to one student, the one student he knew could give the answer he was looking for whilst also getting all the other students to take notice. "Josephine, you got the floor."

She quickly threw her pen down and looked up and around. Everyone in the lecture theatre sat silent, waiting for her response.

She rolled her eyes at the lecturer. They both knew this was amateur hour for her. She took in a big gulp of air and responded, "The Stamping Act, for all intents and purposes, can be seen as ultimately the first act of a government attempting to control the population by deciding who gets to…"

Her train of thought was cut short by a dull sound which filled the theatre. It was the bell and the students needed no further prompting.

The class was over. The entire lecture theatre became a mess of cloud screens as they projected from the eyes of nearly every student, the equivalent of smart phones being ripped out of pockets only a few decades earlier.

In the hallways of the campus, Josephine navigated the student crowds—more students, more Scandinavian chic, more clouds emitting from their eyes. But what was really noticeable was the pace of the crowd; nobody rushed. This wasn't a university campus brimming with frenetic early twenty something energy. There was a buzz but it was different. Nobody here was frantic.

Everyone took their time. Life came to them, unlike life for Kit and Jim and every other Rat who had to chase life. These people understood from birth that the world was built for them, like a rich kid with an inheritance coming to him when he turned eighteen.

A certain amount of ease permeated every facet of their physicality. It bled through in the way they walked, talked and interacted. There was a lightness to the way they operated their day, as if they were gliding around life's hurdles and obstacles, With the ability to harness the latest genetic therapies, and personalized medicine, they were able to maintain optimal health. As a result, the average life expectancy for Clean Skins skyrocketed, reaching one hundred years, solidifying their position at the top of the social hierarchy.

This ease of life was further reinforced by their slim, pixie like body builds—a result of all the inter breeding between other Cleans Skins over the decades.

Another reason why Josephine stood out. Unlike her Clean Skin friends, she moved with purpose. Whilst most of these kids wouldn't pick a career until their early to mid thrities, Josephine already knew her life's purpose. It didn't help that Ignatius Grafton was the most prestigious liberal arts college in the country. It was the reason they were allowed to debate the government's handling of Nox Anima freely. Josephine wondered if the University at large was a tokenistic offering to keep noisy students like her satisfied but also quiet and somewhat contained in a beautifully manicured, self-righteous bubble.

In some way, Josephine's path was pre ordained because of who her father was. In another sense, she was inbuilt with a sense of duty. Maybe it came from her mother. But unfortunately that was something she was never going to find out in her lifetime.

As she dodged and weaved the slow moving students, she mouthed words to herself silently, they had a rhythm to them, as if she were rehearsing a speech...

Outside on the perfect campus gardens, she heard students cheering and a militant voice blaring on a megaphone. Josephine surged towards them and, the closer she got, the more energized she became, priming herself like a performer about to jump on stage to eighty thousand people. She was getting ready to go into battle and whatever headspace she was in, it was fierce.

A skip suddenly appeared in her step. She leaned forward, like an athlete walking down a ramp, her head bobbing up and down. A giant cheer rose as she emerged from the grand ivy colored pillars that lined the outdoor hallway

Signs projected from people's eyes: *Nox Anima, doesn't mean no life*

The focus on Josephine's face was unwavering. She knew not to get caught up in the adulation; it wasn't about that, it was about the fight.

As she made her way through the cheering crowds, random hands burst out and shook her shoulders and patted her on the back—any way to show their appreciation by contact, all of it fuel for what was about to happen next. Skipping up the steps, the MC greeted Josephine with a solemn nod as if to say *They're yours now* before tossing her the microphone.

As her hands touched the microphone, the crowd reached another wave of excitement and cheered louder. Josephine was a pro. She knew the best thing to do was to wait for the excitement to dissipate. Again, it wasn't about the cheering. It was about sending a message and you couldn't get your point across trying to talk over a bunch of riled up students, no matter how supportive they were. She paused. The cheers gradually subsided before a breeze shot through and acted as a calming before the storm, the storm she was about to bring.

"YOU ALL READY FOR A FIGHT?"

The crowd instantly rose again.

"I said, are you ready for a fight?"

Again the crowd let out a raucous chant.

Josephine let the voices wash over her in unison, nodding her head as if to say: *You get me.* She let the rush of support die down again. Taking in a deep breath, she raised her finger and moved the microphone to her mouth. "Thirty years ago, they discovered Nox Anima. Five years later, they introduced the stamping rule. Five years after that, they made it virtually impossible to gain an education…"

Everyone cheered.

"Or vote if you had Nox Anima. Now it's twenty thirty-five, and you can't even have sex with who you want anymore!" The last statement sent the crowd into a collective roar that had most of the nearby students stop what they were doing.

Leaning against one of the ivy colored pillars was Professor Braithewaite. He stood there watching with a small but proud smile. He was old enough to remember a unified society without Nox Anima, so to see someone willing to do everything they could to bring society back brought him a sense of pride, especially when that someone was a Clean Skin, and more so that she was his student.

As the crowd went nuts, Josephine nodded again as if to say: *You get it, you're my people.* Raising her finger once more, she paused, knowing that it would give these final lines the level of gravitas she needed to get these kids to sign up for her cause.

"I'm giving myself a challenge. By twenty forty-five, there will be no *Clean Skins*, no *Rats*. We will not be judged by a stamp we may or may not have on our shoulder. We will not be judged by the length of our names or the time we have on this planet. We will be judged on one thing and one thing alone — Who we are inside. Are you with me!"

The crowd cheered in unison, "Yes!"

Josephine's goal wasn't to handle Nox Anima or even contain it. It was to break it and all those who leveraged off of it. Yet she always battled for credibility, she believed in what she was fighting for but, without the actual blue stamp on her shoulder, there was always an underlying feeling she couldn't shake, and that was she was a poser, a tourist. It was why she got people to call her Jo and not her full Clean Skin name Josephine.

It was classic imposter syndrome. She had the resources, connections and pedigree to take this fight to the top and make a difference. At least she felt like she did, so why not make it her life's work?

But sometimes, when it looked like no progress was being made, she felt as a Rat would say, "pushing shit around a clock." Sometimes she figured maybe it would be better if she quit and left it to someone else. On occasion, when she was truly exhausted, she would look deep within herself and ask, *What do I want to do for the next 80-100 years of my life? I've chosen this, but what if I get it wrong?*

Josephine nodded once more before letting them have her call to action. "Then let's take care of it!"

The crowd exploded.

CHAPTER 4
IT WILL FIND ITS WAY

Jim's car was aggressive and out there, like his personality. A 1980s Ford F-150 with a two tone blue and white metallic paint job sitting atop four self spinning silver rims. It was blinding, scene stealing. It made an entrance as if Liberace had purchased a cowboy truck and asked Xzibit to pimp his ride. This wasn't just a way to get from A to B. This car, like a Rat's clothes, home, body and tattoos, was an extension of himself—wear everything on the outside because that was what people saw first, that was the way of the Rat.

Jim sat casually in the driver's seat, one arm hanging out the window. Kit sat in the passenger seat staring outside at the problems that plagued the city. Gun stores followed by liquor stores followed by pawn shops, shop fronts you'd never see on the Clean Skin side of town. All these cash businesses circulating money and violence between them in a never ending cycle of self destruction.

Kit recalled a quote from Furious Styles when he snuck in and watched Boyz N the Hood with some older kids when he was younger. "The quickest way to destroy a people is you take away their ability to reproduce themselves."

The final image probably summed up the neighborhood most succinctly, a row of Rats kneeling on the curb being handcuffed and patted down by the police… most likely just for being themselves.

Kit had had enough and turned back to Jim, who was now juggling the wheel whilst trying to put on the gaudy gold watch he stole from the dead man's apartment. Kit grabbed the wheel.

Jim nodded in appreciation. "Thanks."

Even for Kit, this act surprised him. "You really took his watch?"

Jim waved him off. "Mine's scuffed and plus, all the toy dinosaurs were taken." He smirked, proud of his comeback. "I bet that Clean Skin you snuffed out won't do a day in jail, it's all for show… I bet they let her go the moment they turned the corner."

Kit couldn't help but shrug in agreement but he knew it really wasn't about her. "And the baby?" he asked in the most innocuous manner.

Jim finished putting his new watch on before taking a few moments to hold it up and admire it whilst grabbing the wheel again. "It will find its way."

The comment shocked Kit. He looked at Jim for an inordinate amount of time hoping his glare would change his mind, but it didn't. "Dude… It's a baby man." His voice soaked in that similar disbelief that his glare was giving off.

"Then you adopt it!" Jim arched back throwing up an arm as if to say: *Why is this our problem?*

Kit went silent but didn't take his gaze off Jim. He wanted him to know he was being a heartless prick.

Jim, deep down, didn't want to disappoint his best friend with some callous comment. "It'll survive. Like we did. That's why they call us Rats, even if we're racing against time, you can never really get rid of us." He hoped his comment would smooth over his previous aggressive response.

There was a silence between the two. Kit wasn't entirely happy with Jim's answer but also aware that their world was what it was, and there was no changing it. Both grappled with the fact that the older they got in this life, the fewer people they had to rely on.

Kit had already lost someone close to him. The next question after a death was always, "Who's next?"

Deep down, without wanting to speak the words out loud, both knew, all they actually had was each other until one of them started showing their red cross on their shoulder,

But that day wasn't today, so it was best that they got over their beef on this matter and got back to racing against time.

Jim looked back at Kit quickly, then back to the road. A wry smile crept over his face. "So… we going to visit your girlfriend?"

CHAPTER 5
WILL YOU GO OUT
WITH ME?

Inside a cavernous, decaying church, Josephine had set up a trestle table full of chips, soda, carrot sticks, dips, fruit and anything else a child would eat at recess. She checked her watch before moving over and straightening the chairs that had been arranged in a circle.

A large clunking sound echoed and brought with it a wave of pre teens in that chaotic maelstrom of chatter, laughter and yelling. Josephine spun around as this sea of ten and twelve year olds washed past her and headed straight for the food. Some threw up a fist for her to bump; others nodded at her, and some ignored her.

If the rallies where a way of mobilizing those who could make a difference, this work here in the trenches was a way for her to gain a first hand insight into a world she really only understood in theory.

Like a pack of locusts descending on a corn field, the kids marauded the table as if it was their last meal on earth. For most of them, it was their last meal for the day. Majority of them were from broken homes, one parent households, and some had no parents at all. These were the forgotten kids of society, kids as Jim had said earlier, were left to find their way.

But you wouldn't have known it from the banter and ribbing. The politics of the schoolyard remained and continued amidst mouthfuls of chips and soda. Whilst some kids wore long sleeve t-shirts, others wore singlets and their blue stamp was visible for all to see. Being kids, there was an obliviousness to their plight, as if they didn't even know they had Nox Anima or were stamped—that was until they were forced to talk about it.

Moments later, Josephine had all ten kids sitting around in a circle. The chatter continued but now, with full stomachs, they were somewhat better focused and satiated.

Josephine doled out more cups of soda. "So I have a question I've been meaning to ask you guys."

Some of the kids rolled their eyes. It was the typical start to one of these gatherings.

Don, a twelve-year-old going on twenty-one, whose face had seen way too much for his young life, threw up a lazy hand.

"Yes, Don," Josephine said, her tone implying she already knew what the question was going to be.

"Will you go out with me?"

The line sent the group into hysterics. Don already

knew the answer, what he was looking for was the response, and he got it. He sat back, trying to send his most seductive look to Josephine, but she was too old and too busy for that.

"When you're older, Don," Josephine said in her most neutral voice without skipping a beat. As she continued to pour the kids their sodas, she looked up. "Guys we're losing track here, My question is, has anyone here imagined themselves with more time?"

The question, as existential as it was, and maybe even a bit too mature for them, had sent all of these youngsters into a self reflective silence, and that was exactly what Josephine wanted. It was a sign she was getting through to them, but also a sign that someone was listening and wanted to know more. That someone from the other side actually cared. But as the silence continued, Josephine wondered if the question was too much.

She was about to pivot when a meek voice came from the other side of the circle. "I did."

The answer had come from Mil, a twelve-year-old girl, who looked like she had raised herself but also spoke only when she had something to say.

The chatter raised the moment Mil gave her answer.

"Guys shussh!" Josephine pleaded. "Mil, tell us how you did that?"

Mil looked at everyone in the circle. To her she was

putting herself out there. Nox Anima kids were savage, a wrong answer and they would pile on top of her, but Mil thought for a moment, then shrugged to herself. "I colored over my shoulder stamp with make up. Then I imagined myself with seventy years."

Josephine nodded and pointed and mouthed the word "Good" in a bid to make sure Mil felt she had done the right thing in sharing. The answer had turned the entire circle of kids silent. More importantly, it had got them thinking. These were those moments that nourished Josephine and kept her fighting.

"So what does everyone think of that? How did that make you feel?"

Mil thought about it again and weighed her words carefully for a twelve-year-old. "It made me feel good, but then the longer I imagined it, the sadder I got because I realized it wasn't real."

Seconds passed as Josephine waited for what was hopefully the beginning of a dialogue.

"Fuck that." Don waved. "I'd be imagining one hundred years. And I'd be using one of them signal jammers too."

The term "signal jammer" sent the entire room of kids into a full blown spin. It was a piece of tech only talked about in hushed tones because nobody in real life had ever actually seen one. The kids argued over one another, competing with recollecting stories about when they may have encountered the mythical piece of technology.

"Where you getting a signal jammer?" Mil questioned Don. "You're twelve years old." Mil seeing through his bullshit sent the entire group into hysterics.

"Hey get fucked!" Don snarled back.

This was par for the course for Josephine. Keeping these kids focused was ninety percent of the battle. She had a sense when she had totally lost them and today was one of those days.

"Guys! Guys! Can we settle down?"

Rex, another kid who didn't have the smarts of Mil or the confidence of Don, raised his hand amidst the chaos.

"Yes, Rex." Josephine pointed.

"Miss Jo. Is it true you only here with us because it makes you feel better about yourself?" Rex's face was serious but also inquisitive. He didn't know he was asking an offensive question. To him, it was just a question.

Josephine got the focus she required from the group again but unfortunately not the desired topic. She took a moment, as the question took the wind out of her. With one innocent question, this child had managed to rock the core values which she thought made her a good person. Here she was, a Clean Skin, donating her time in a bid to help them realize that they too were worthy of love, respect and time.

Yet the question had sucked all the air out of the room and sent the kids into a pause that demanded an answer. They all looked at Josephine. She felt naked in front of them. There was no way she could dig her way out, but at the same time, a look of incredulity came over her, and more importantly, the need to know where this question came from.

"Who told you that?"

"My older cousin," Rex responded.

"Tell him he's wrong." Her answer was short, sharp and laced with a finality not usually reserved for these poor kids.

Rex quietly nodded, both aware he was going to relay her response back to his cousin later.

Bam raised his hand.

Josephine was now exhausted by the exchange. "Yes, Bam, what do you want?"

"Can we watch a movie from your cloud?"

Defeated, Josephine took a long blink. "Sure, okay fine."

The kids in unison all hissed *Yessssss!* Josephine knew the session was as good as over tonight. It was one of those nights where she would cut her losses and try and find the one or two positives amongst it all. Today, it was the rally at the campus so she felt somewhat okay to take it easy tonight.

Josephine pushed the button that sat behind the lobe

of her ear and her screen emerged from her eye. It was the first time she had activated her OurCloud since this morning. She sat there as a menu popped up on screen not unlike a Netflix catalogue of movies. The kids yelled as they blurted out their suggestions over one another until Josephine chose a movie tile and selected it. It was almost always a comedy movie, something for ninety minutes that could help them forget about their day, their week, but mostly their life. As the opening credits rolled and the kids settled down, Josephine sat there and wondered if she was really making the difference she desired.

CHAPTER 6
ACROSS THE WINDOW

Jim and Kit had pulled up on the curb. Kit got out.

Jim smiled at him. "You could actually try talking to her this time."

Kit rolled his eyes. "And what am I going to say?"

Jim shrugged. "I don't know, my name is Kit and I like pottery… please have sex with me before I die."

Kit threw up his middle finger and slammed the door before he made his way to the back of the pickup and slid over a box. Running his finger through the cheap plastic items inside, he took one last look at the assortment of kids' toys. The trinkets ranged from handheld video game consoles to jewelry to hats and headphones. All of them had been collected and chucked in the box by the removalists over the course of a day. It was their way of giving back to the community. Mostly it was tokenistic and made Kit sometimes wonder whether encouraging the value of these things to the next generation just perpetuated problematic Rat culture. That the only thing that mattered in their world was what you owned and how you looked. Again, similar to an actual real life Rat, jogging on a spinning wheel of consumption.

Kit walked through the creaking, wooden doors. The church was barely lit. It was cool inside, a handy by-product of being built in bluestone many centuries ago. The blurred sounds of a movie could be heard through the glass doors that separated the main church from the reception area.

Kit crept up with his box. He leaned his head looking to get a glimpse of the woman who was always here with the kids. Reaching the glass, he lowered the box of toys and took a moment. There she was… Josephine and the youths all watching the movie being projected from her OurCloud screen.

Kit didn't know what he liked about Josephine. The cold hard truth was he didn't know her. In fact, he didn't know any Clean Skins except for his Nan, and technically you couldn't be called a Clean Skin if you were born before the discovery of Nox Anima. Was it the fact that Josephine hung out with Rats? Maybe it was that willingness to reach out to the other side that humanized her, made her interesting, made her approachable.

If she was so approachable then why couldn't he just approach her? Or maybe it was the opposite? The fact she had the guts to venture over here every week made her impossible to approach, someone out of his league.

A succession of loud blares came from outside. Kit looked behind him. The spell was broken. Jim threw up his hands and, in no uncertain terms, motioned for Kit to *hurry the f--- up!*

Kit turned around and left whilst Josephine remained. The sound of the clunk of the door made her pause the movie and turn around. The kids all jeered in unison asking what the hell was going on. Josephine looked back but Kit had already disappeared. Turning back around, she reanimated her OurCloud, and as quickly as the movie started playing, the kids fell silent again.

The entire day for Josephine had been a succession of leaps from one social engagement to the next. She hadn't touched the ground since she woke up this morning, and now, she was waiting at a restaurant for some random guy to arrive. She was mentally and emotionally tapped out and this date was the thing she was looking forward to the least.

Yet it was easier to go through with it than put it off another five times. Elizabeth, her best friend, was adamant she needed someone in her life to soften up her hard edges. Josephine would rather just find someone who could handle them or, easier yet, not bother with anyone at all.

The restaurant itself resonated with a civilized

hum—far more muted than your typical fine dining eatery. Chill wave music played over the speakers and perfectly complimented the light-colored timber that carefully lined the walls and the ceiling. The place resembled the inside of a guitar. Josephine had grabbed a booth.

She was wearing a different configuration of that Scandinavian look. Her mind was somewhere else, on her work. It would take someone pretty damn special to take her attention away from her life's ambition. In her mind she had already put in too much effort for this guy and changed her clothes twice. This wasn't really the kind of person she was, so she already felt she wasn't projecting her true self.

Checking her watch one more time, she let out a frustrated sigh and reached behind her ear when suddenly she spotted a guy entering from the other side. Tall, waifish, dressed similarly to herself. He sent a polite smile and nod her way before glad-handing a few people.

Josephine was none too impressed. He was late to their date and now making her wait some more. She smiled back and pretended it didn't bother her. It was clear this was his attempt to prove his value in a social setting, but all it proved was that he was a selfish dick who bought into the bullshit of their world.

A few minutes later he reached her side of the restaurant. Christian was twenty-five and was better looking up close, which pissed her off even more, as it made him seem entitled. If anything, he was more of a boy than a man. In fact, most Clean Skin men resembled boys. It was their limited understanding of the greater world by keeping it at arm's length and not getting themselves dirty or messy. This extended not only to how they dressed but how they handled their emotions and their lack of self-awareness and vulnerability. Bizarrely, they wore all this as some sort of badge of honor as if they were undamaged by the frailties of humanity. Something about picturing this boy attempt some form of physical labor made her laugh inside.

"Hey, hope you didn't start without me." He attempted to play off his tardiness with a joking tone.

All Josephine could offer was a forced smile as he sat.

He sat there looking her up and down and gave some weird nod. "You look different from your profile."

Josephine didn't know how to respond and reached behind her ear, scratching around her OurCloud button she decided against it and instead offered a tired sigh. "What were you expecting?"

No doubt, tonight was going to be a long night.

Time had passed and somehow Josephine had made it through the main course with this boy. His body language said it all—one leg crossed over the other, sitting at an angle away from Josephine with his wine glass out swirling around.

"It's cute you know," he started.

Josephine screwed up her face. "What is?"

Christian smirked. "You folks, with your protests and all, trying to fix Nox Anima."

Josephine's face immediately turned to stone. He didn't even look at her after making his statement. He swirled his wine before looking back expecting his comment to start some sort of robust conversation.

All Josephine wanted to do was reach over the table and smash the wine glass over his stupid face. She suppressed her rage but kept her face frozen. "I think it got beyond cute a long time ago."

Christian shrugged his shoulders in a way that signified he didn't really care either way. "Well let's be honest, we could eliminate Nox Anima in fifty years if we just stopped them from breeding with each other."

Josephine looked around, wondering if anyone else was hearing what this idiot was saying. "So, on top of all the rights they already have had stripped, you now want to stop them from having sex with each other? Tell me again, what do you do for a living?"

His chuckle came across as condescending. "That question is so overdone these days, don't you think?"

Josephine returned serve right away. "Not if that something you do is something that needs to be done."

Christian sighed. "Very well, I don't do anything."

Josephine half expected that answer. "And that doesn't bother you?"

"Why should it? I have approximately one hundred years of life expectancy and enough cloud credit not to care."

"Sounds like you have it all figured out," Josephine said with a resignation in her voice. It wasn't about salvaging the date anymore, it was about teaching this imbecile some empathy, or better yet humility.

"I don't have it figured out… that's why I'm living my life and you're still wasting yours trying to cure a mutation that went out of fashion when your father did."

Now she was ready to glass this asshole.

Christian didn't flinch. "It's not an insult, Josephine. It's an invitation. This is the real world for us, and I've just come to terms with it quicker than most. Question is would you be ready to join me?"

Josephine had no response and wasn't prepared to give one. She had had enough of this dickhead. He was about to say something else when she reached for the back of her ear and pressed her OurCloud button. A screen glitched and Christian and the restaurant vanished in a chaotic mix of digital noise and pixels.

Josephine sat up in her bed in her pajamas inside her dorm. Gone was the restaurant, Christian, the chill wave music and timber surroundings. The date was a virtual one via the OurCloud interface and in this day and age as good as the real thing. Or as bad.

Josephine nodded and fell back onto her bed. "What a dipshit."

CHAPTER 7
F--- THEM, THAT'S WHY

Sped up Top 40 pop music with sexualized overtones blared over the speakers and punched bursts of sound through the lasers and artificial haze. Through all the chaos, barely visible half naked men and women could be seen gyrating and grinding, their blue iridescent shoulder stamps glowing even brighter under the black light of the strip club in a weird sensual dance.

When Nox Anima arrived three decades prior, it had some unforeseen side effects. One of those was the elimination of the divides such as race, sex, orientation and religion. Overnight they all disappeared and were replaced by one single element: time. You either had it or you didn't and nothing else mattered, so in actual fact, all known prejudice was really just bundled up into one neat little package. As the world grew more efficient so did the way people expressed discrimination.

Some of the strippers sported faint red crosses inside their stamps, others had red crosses far more prominent and it was clear from their physical appearance, that soon, their time would be up. Men and women surrounded them, using their own hard earned cash to make it rain dollar bills and cheer them on, hoping to score private lap dances.

In the corner, in a booth, alone, away from the music, lights and naked bodies, Jim and Kit hoed into a bunch of steaks. To them they might as well have been eating these meals at a regular diner. Whatever was happening on stage was of no interest to them. They were more hungry than horny. Kit looked up and clocked Kel; everything about her was fake—fake boobs, fake lips, hair extensions, contacts that gave her eyes a dazzling green luster, and a covering of tattoos that only stopped to accentuate the bits that people came to the club to see. She winked at Kit and he in turn offered a polite nod.

Jim looked back. He turned to Kit. "You haven't slept with her yet?"

Kit could only wave him off in response.

Tai waltzed in, half naked, her head bopping to the beat. A woman who was always in motion, she was half Asian, but unlike a lot of the men and women here, didn't see the need to bolster her body with implants, fillers and silicone. Those things were more so a product of Rat culture than stripper culture.

Regardless Tai was still quite striking, although the rash climbing up her arm and the faint red cross within her stamp had become more noticeable than anything else.

Jim immediately grabbed her arm and inspected her cross. He ran his fingers over it. "It's looking darker."

She whipped her arm back. "It's fine." She took a seat and nestled in next to Jim.

The two of them had been a couple for the last seven years, a rarity in Rat society. Jim had met Tai in the club after a lap dance and had instantly fell in love. She was homeless at the time and had lost her parents at an early age so really didn't know what family was. All Jim wanted to do from that point was give her the life she deserved and Tai was more than happy to be taken care of for the first time in her life. From then on, every year they fell more and more in love.

Tai stole a few fries from Jim's plate and motioned to Kit with a mouthful of fried potato. "So did you tell Kit?"

"Tell me what?"

Jim sat there with a proud and mischievous smile.

Kit couldn't read him. "What? Tell me what?"

Jim looked around before digging into his pocket and producing a small circular contraption. It sat on the table. It was smooth, donut shaped and made of a shiny aluminum alloy with a blinking light on the underside.

Kit looked around and then looked back at Jim and

Tai, his mouth agape. Nothing more needed to be said, but Kit was going to say it anyway, "Is that a…"

Jim interrupted immediately. "You bet your Nan it is."

Kit picked it up and studied it. "Where the hell you get a signal jammer from?" His voice remained hushed and conspiratorial.

Jim shrugged and smiled, as if to say: *I have my ways.*

Kit weighed it in his hand. It was heavier than it looked, a good sign. It meant that it was filled with top notch components and circuitry. Nobody knew where the first jammer came from or who made it, but it was assumed it was something anguished over by a brilliant but troubled neuroscience genius who probably lived in a basement somewhere, scared of the outside world or maybe disgusted as to what it had become. This person's invention was their humble contribution to tearing down the wall that kept these two societies apart.

Kit looked at Jim again. "So what are you going to do with it?"

"What aren't we going to do with it?" Jim smirked back.

"I'll tell you what we're going to do with it." Tai shot back. "Hit up that college party, Clean Skins only.

"Why?" Kit asked.

Everyone knew Rats hosted the best parties. It came with the territory. The math was simple. They partied the hardest because they had nothing to lose.

"Fuck em that's why." Tai's response was sharp and direct, like a war cry, a call to action. What she was really saying was: *You can't exclude us from society. We are just as much a part of it as you are, and just because you were dealt a better hand doesn't make you a better person.*

Kit handed back the Jammer and looked to his two best friends. "Well then we're going to need some new clothes."

CHAPTER 8
YOU KNOW WHAT
THEY SAY

Kit got dressed. He was in his underpants, and for the first time, you could see his stamp and his body. He was in good shape and his stamp stood out like everyone else's. He was no different even if it was becoming clear that he was more self reflective and interior than most other Rats.

Kel was next to him. She was doing the same and putting herself back together. Both were silent. They had just had sex—whether the sex was any good was anyone's guess, but in their world, sex was there to be had. Just another pleasure outlet in a world where you could be gone any moment.

The bathroom didn't add much to the atmosphere. It was grimy, walled out with dirty mirrors caked with make up and tiles that needed a blasting with an industrial pressure hose. The music from the strip stage penetrated the walls but not enough to hear the lyrics, just the incessant throbbing of the bass.

Kit's wallet had fallen to the ground as he shimmied

himself into his ripped jeans.

Kel was quick to notice as it had opened up on a transparent slip that housed a photo of a woman. She slowly picked it up and studied the photo before handing it back over. "You going back to her tonight?"

Kit was surprised she had it. He looked around as if it was still lost or that she had picked his pocket. It took him a moment, but he finally responded in a solemn tone. "She's dead."

Monogamy wasn't common amongst Rats. Why limit yourself to one person when you could sleep with anyone and everyone and know they would be doing the same? This lifestyle even had its own motto: "LIFL: Love Is For Losers." It was one of the OG movements when Nox Anima had finally become common place. But again Kit was different, and recently a new movement had begun that saw a lot of Rats pairing up as they approached their mid twenties. It was as much as a decision based on fear as it was reflection and acceptance.

Nobody wanted to die alone, and the odds of having your friends still alive when your time was up were low.

It wasn't the answer Kel was expecting. In fact the answer had changed the temperature in the room immediately to something somber. Kit looked up and could now see the pity on Kel's face. "That's interesting," she said with a curious tone in her voice.

"What is?" Kit didn't care but now was a moment to be polite.

"That you had a girlfriend."

Kit shook his head. "I'm just sick of this whole LIFL thing."

Kel now shook her head. "But love *is*… love is for losers, at least in our world."

Kit threw on his t-shirt and snatched his wallet from Kel. "Our world is their world, Kel, there just happens to be a wall dividing it. Doesn't mean we don't deserve what they have." On that note, he left Kel there to ponder his closing remark.

The door swung open letting in a rush of light, music, and haze before closing again, leaving Kel to look at herself in the mirror and wonder if maybe he had a point.

CHAPTER 9
THAT'S THEIR JOB...
TO DIE

A sunset sky and the orange tinted clouds passed over at pace behind a glass window. The vision was accompanied by music—easy, slow going, calming, almost ethereal. Josephine watched all this go by. She lay on her back deep in thought in the back seat of a self driving car. The car itself was clean and pristine—white, tasteful light oak finishing on the dashboard complimented by cream leather trim on the seats. If a car could dress like a Clean Skin, this would be it. It wasn't so much a car as a lounge room that moved.

Outside the passenger windows, houses floated by, each one grand but not ostentatious, cream-colored brickwork, clean lines, and manicured gardens but nothing that would draw the eye. A Clean Skin house didn't draw attention because it didn't have to. It was confident in itself and its place in the world. People chatted, kids rode bikes and scooters—it wasn't fake, it wasn't even controlled... it was simply oblivious. The differences between what Kit had witnessed out of his window and what Josephine saw out of hers (when she wasn't deep in thought) couldn't be more different.

A pleasant alert chime from the onboard computer filled the space of the car's cabin, alerting Josephine to an incoming call.

"Call from Elizabeth," the car said in a pleasant older female voice.

Josephine took a deep sigh, her energy not ready for what was about to come. She pressed her cloud button behind her ear and out projected her screen, and her friend, Elizabeth Rich. One thing Elizabeth had was excitement. It exuded out of every pore of her body. It came through her smile, eyes and the sing song quality in the voice, which at times could ramp up to an imperceptible speed when she got truly excited. It was a product of her never having faced any adversity. It didn't make her conceded; it just made her unaware. She wanted people to catch her zest but didn't really have the empathy to understand why people carried baggage—because she had none.

Her father was a famous architect, and her mother ran some of the biggest charities in the city and both thought the world of her. She was studying architecture like her father but would probably change to marketing or business by the end of semester. She considered her best friend Josephine a bit of a project. She felt it was her duty to open this person to the sunnier things in life. In her mind that made her a loyal friend.

"Hey, what the hell happened with you and Christian? He told me one minute you were getting along and having great conversation and then suddenly you buttoned off on him."

Josephine shook her head. "Is that what he told you?"

Elizabeth nodded. "Yeah, he said it was going great and then you just went all rude on him."

Josephine scoffed. She couldn't believe this was how he had perceived the date, but then again self awareness was rare amongst Clean Skin boys. "Let's just say that we would never have worked out and I was doing him a favor."

Elizabeth shrugged. "Last time I set you up."

Josephine scoffed again and chuckled. "I doubt that very much."

Elizabeth's face lightened as they both saw the levity in the situation. "Well why don't we try looking for guys the old fashioned way and go to this party on Saturday."

Josephine waved her head in a non comital sway. Unless it was tied to a cause, or a rally, Josephine wasn't the most social person. She found the conversations at these parties never went any deeper than the basics—career, education, holidays. Rarely did she exit one of these gatherings feeling intellectually nourished let alone inspired or surprised.

"I'll think about it," she said knowing that again it

may be easier to attend than say no, at least it meant she wouldn't have to attend another for another two months. "I'll talk to you later."

Josephine pressed her cloud button and sent her screen projection back into her eye. She sat up and looked out the window. The car approached her family's house. It came to a graceful stop and the door magically opened in a gullwing fashion. Josephine stepped out, and the door closed again automatically behind her. Something made her childhood home stand out from the others, and not in a good way. The house was tired, the garden was unkept, the paint peeling, the windows murky. Her father never ventured outside. He was the man who first discovered Nox Anima, the man who the world's hope had rested upon.

Josephine let herself in, the echo of her keys navigating the barrels of the door locks bounced around the smooth plastered walls of the house's grand entrance. Again, this place would have been impressive twenty years ago, but now, it was just the memory of a home. She closed the door and put away her own set of keys whilst calling out for her father. No response. She heard faint laughter and chatter though.

Josephine's shoulders dropped and she rubbed her face. She knew exactly what that meant and it wasn't good. Walking towards the sounds, she passed a giant photo frame that hung by the stairs. It was a family portrait, taken years ago—a mother, father and two twin girls, age four, dressed in matching floral dresses. Bizarrely, none of them dressed like Scandinavians. Obviously from another time, a time when the world was a little more integrated.

The sounds grew louder, making it clear that the chatter was that of children. Josephine sidled up to the doorway. In a dimly lit living room, her father sat on a couch watching what looked like home movies. He was a sad version of the proud upright man in the photo frame—the man with the sparkly eyes that was interviewed thirty years ago on Prime Time TV. Montgomery Dunn slumped on the couch, nursing a drink. He was all round shoulders and five o'clock shadow, so in his own world that he had no idea Josephine was watching him from the doorway.

On the screen, the two twins and their mother from the portrait played and laughed. Montgomery chatted to them as if the moment was happening in real time. The technology embedded in it had an element of interaction that allowed him to feel like he was there and those on screen to respond to him in some rudimentary fashion. Josephine watched as her father interacted with Hazeldine Dunn, her mother, and her sister Beverline.

Beverline ran right up to the screen. Josephine took notice; she rarely took time to think about her twin sister much anymore. They were both young when she and her mother died in a car crash and Josephine refused to get lost in the world of memory bots like her father had. She had heard stories of people losing sight of what was real and what was not. The memory bots became so real that they blurred the lines of reality and ultimately turned ordinary people into zombies stuck in a moment in time, unwilling to leave. The most extreme of these cases had seen people starve to death from lack of self care.

The video began glitching and Beverline kept repeating the same phrase over "Hey Dad" over and over again — the illusion of Beverline being with them shattered by the limitation of the technology. Montgomery cursed and voice commanded the memory bot to reset. Josephine was thankful her father couldn't afford the latest Membot software upgrade that eliminated the glitches. She took the opportunity to walk away before her father noticed she'd been spying on him.

The refrigerator door was open. Taped to the door was a faded magazine cover with Montgomery Dunn in a suit with no tie standing proud, eyes serious. The title read: *He discovered Nox Anima, now can he cure it?* The eyes had been scratched out, no doubt by Montgomery himself.

Josephine grabbed some ingredients and set them down on the table. She closed a glass panel over the food items, and a set of robotic hands went to work creating dinner.

Josephine called out to her father, "Dinner will be ready in ten minutes."

Moments later, Montgomery emerged. He had put on a cardigan and, somehow, its loose-fitting lack of structure made him appear even more depressed. He sat down quietly with Josephine at the kitchen bench, and the food was there ready for him on his plate. A combination of rice, vegetables, greens and nuts, arranged in an aesthetically pleasing manner in the bowl. Eating healthy was still the one thing she could get her father to do.

Taking a seat, he offered a grateful thanks. The two began eating and, for the first few mouthfuls, it was quiet.

Montgomery took a moment before asking, "So what's been going on?"

His question felt obligatory. He loved Josephine, but the compounded weight of the fatal car crash, coupled with his global failure, was so crushing that it tainted every action, word and thought he had. According to Montgomery, he had failed the world, so the world took away his wife and a daughter.

"Well I had a session with the kids from the Flats."

"I don't know why you waste your time with those Rat kids."

Josephine shook her head. "I don't know why you waste your time with those memory bots."

Montgomery had no comeback for that. The two continued eating. This exchange was not foreign to either of them—one of them was full of hope and at the beginning of their journey to change the world, the other was at their end and realized the world was indifferent and didn't care what plans you had. Yet they could never meet in the middle during dinner time.

Josephine couldn't remember when her father became this guy. As with all things, it happened gradually, then all at once.

She took a few more mouthfuls but something didn't sit right. "And don't call them Rats… I can't help these people if I don't understand them. If I'm not the difference, who is? Remember who told me that?"

Montgomery produced a weird *pfft* sound somewhat impressed and proud that his daughter was using his own life slogan against him in a discussion.

"What's to understand, they're dying, that's their job."

The lack of humanity in Montgomery's voice was shocking, but nothing Josephine hadn't heard before. She was used to the defeat in his approach, but that never stopped her from wanting to try and drag him back from the abyss.

"Maybe if you didn't have that attitude you would have done your job in the first place."

Montgomery stood up and took his plate. "It's not my fault Nox Anima exists. I did more than anyone on this planet and failed, but that's how it goes sometimes. It seems you're the one who is still struggling to let go." Walking back into the lounge room, he called back out to her, "Make sure you're here Saturday. I need help cleaning the study. Thanks for dinner by the way."

Josephine threw up her hands. "I was about to make dessert."

It was too late. He was already gone. He'd disappeared into some private space in the house.

Josephine leaned back and threw her napkin on the table in resignation. "What a pain in the ass."

She looked at her wrist at the faded friendship bracelet; its color had receded into the lackluster duller tones of yellow, purple and green. It was the first gift her twin sister had given her when they were four and it was the last one too. The thing was now over twenty years old and had had its clasps replaced more times than she could remember. But it was one of her few tangible connections to her family. It meant more to her now than ever as her father slowly slipped further and further down the ladder.

CHAPTER 10
THAT WAS A JOKE

Kit's apartment was a strange blend of neatness and chaos, high art and low income. It looked way too nice inside to be simply one of the many hundreds of apartments that were squeezed into the tower blocks in the Flats. There was something timeless about the furnishings, the art, the paint on the walls—almost as if he wasn't the only one living there. Not only that, soft music was playing, and the sound of a machine, a low hum, kept repeating, like a metal disk spinning and grinding on a stationary metal plate.

Stepping inside, Kit felt beat, tired from a day of removing dead Rats' stuff. It was not only physically taxing but mentally draining, especially witnessing something as harrowing as what he witnessed that morning.

Weirdly it was a first in all his years, not entirely uncommon, but a first for him. He couldn't stop thinking about it—the woman's screams, the way she clawed back at the cupboard, the way her body had seized up. He wondered what would be worse, to be released and live with the fact that your Rat baby would grow up alone wandering the streets or to be put in Rat jail and possibly never make it out alive. The stories coming out from Rat jail were like those from Central American prisons, which had been overtaken and were now run by the inmates.

Heading right for the kitchen, he opened the fridge, grabbed a can of whip cream and shot it right into his mouth, before sticking it back in and then smashing a handful of day old French fries. When he opened the bin to throw out the package, something halted his movement. Leaning in, he took out what looked like a plastic pre-scription bottle: *Donepezil: To treat all stages of Alzheimer's.* Kit dropped his shoulders and sighed out the word fuck. "Nan!"

"In here," she called back. Her response was gentle, the voice of someone who never raised their tone or saw the need to.

Kit's shoulders dropped again but this time in relief.

Following the music and the repeated low hum, Kit entered the lounge room to find Nan manning a pottery wheel. His grandmother was his only known relative. His father's mother was born in a time before Nox Anima and now, at the age of seventy, was showing signs of Alzheimer's and was confined to a wheelchair. Her hair was white yet still thick and she had a warmth to her that made you want to tell her everything.

With the last of the sun beaming through the window, she looked angelic. She didn't dress like a Clean Skin, and definitely not like a Rat, but like someone who didn't know the rules of the new world. She was stuck out of time but knew more than she let on.

Since the rise of Nox Anima, Nan watched the world lean heavily toward the youth and their culture and the only question ever asked now was: *How much time you have left or how much time you've got?* To her, life had become about potential; nobody cared about the aftermath or the wisdom you had acquired.

Kit held up the prescription bottle. "Hey, Nan, what are these?"

She quickly glanced over not wanting to lose focus on the bowl she was forming with her hands. "I guess I forgot."

Kit raised his eyebrows, it was hard to be mad at this woman.

Nan offered back a cheeky smile. "That was a joke."

"Yeah, it is until it's not." Kit remained unimpressed to make his point.

Nan motioned her head over to the couch. On it, lay a red dress. "I found that in my stuff."

Kit walked over and held it up. The dress was definitely of the Rat type—tight fitting, out there, a real statement piece. Kit swallowed hard. The dress was stirring things inside him.

"You want me to send it to goodwill?" Nan enquired.

Kit didn't respond immediately. "No, it's Gems. I'll take care of it." He breathed in deeply, channeling his emotions, or worse yet, suppressing them. "I'm just gonna go to my room."

Kit's room was a little more in the style synonymous with a Rat, shabby but chic. The room was full but not bursting with material goods like most Rats. The one thing they had going for them is that their cash economy kept most goods at a steady price as it was always the same money circulating within the population, It was the one insulation they had against the Clean Skin's cloud credit and debt that was always looking to upend the global economy. He pulled the toy dinosaur out of his pocket, and tossed it inside a bowl next to his bed full of other random trinkets, each one of them from a house he had done removal work on. Having watched these people have their entire lives and memories pillaged made him realize that they should respect the memories. Keeping a piece of each house was his way of making sure their life remained way beyond their use by date, even if it was in the form of a toy dinosaur.

He opened his closet, brushed his clothes to one side of the rack, and put Gem's dress up to his nose and breathed it in. Her scent was called Rose and smelt just like that with a dash of pepper. Whatever was left of her scent traveled up his nasal passage and took him back to a time when she was the only thing that mattered in his life. He opened his eyes slowly, her presence still with him. Respectfully he hung the red dress on the other side. He stared at it for a moment before heading to his bed and searching underneath. Seconds later, he produced a shoe box. He sat down and opened it, revealing a wad of cash. Pulling out some more notes from his pocket, he added to the wad and then wrote down the amount he had earned today in a ledger - three hundred dollars. The total amount was getting close to twenty thousand dollars now.

Sitting amongst all this was a brochure for a retirement home. There was no way around it. When Nox Anima finally came calling for him, it would be too late. He knew his only hope to give Nan some semblance of a normal life was to send her to a decent retirement home before he died. God knew she was too stubborn to send herself, so ever since Kit could make money, he saved it. It was why he had less than everyone else— less clothes, less jewelry, less everything. It was all being saved for Nan.

But in a way it made him free. He was who he was regardless of what he wore and owned and what Rat society demanded of him.

Kit made his way to the bathroom, taking off his shirt. He opened the drawer and took out a pair of hair clippers. He flicked it on and the device produced a rattling electric buzz. Setting himself down in his bath, he got himself comfortable before he started the process of shaving his own head. Clumps of hair fell over his face. Unlike his friends, Kit was not going to spend money on a fresh weekly cut when he could put that money towards Nan.

For a brief moment, he stopped and thought about Gem. She used to shave his head. She'd sit on the edge of the bath, his head between her legs. It was as intimate as any sex they'd had, plus she could also give him a fade, something he was not able to do very well on his own.

He turned off the razor. That peppery rose scent was still in his nostrils. He froze. He wondered what Gem would think about the Jammer. Knowing her, she most likely would not have joined them at the party. Rat parties were rarely her scene let alone crashing a Clean Skin one. She was the opposite of most of the women out there that he had dated, she was deep, thoughtful and challenged him, it was a combination of personality he had struggled to find since her death.

Suddenly there was a beep. It was his phone. He found a message from Jim *We need your clothing size so Tai can suit you up for the party, make sure it's correct, we're not exactly built the same as them.*

CHAPTER 11
BE THE DIFFERENCE

Somewhere in a random university campus bathroom, Kit, Tai and Jim stood in front of the large mirror. Dressed like Clean Skins they looked weird to say the least, their muscular, toned bodies too defined for the clothes that Tai had sourced for them. Kit sported loose fitting beige chino's with the cuffs rolled up and shoes that were clearly Common Project knock offs. His jumper was dark brown, and he had rolled his sleeves up very slightly.

Jim wore grey pleated pants with similar shoes and a loose fitting off pale blue shirt that was left untucked. He finished off his look with a grey cardigan.

Tai also wore pants but hers were charcoal and pleated, her shirt was white, loose fitting but tucked in, her belt was simple but tasteful and her jacket was thin, cream and sat loosely over her.

Kit inspected his outfit. "They're going to see right through us."

Tai nodded her head silently. "Nah, they're not, we just gotta wear it like we own it."

Clean Skins by default would rarely visit the gym. Self improvement was like a form of masturbation to them—it meant you weren't confident in yourself because something needed to be fixed, unlike a Rat who was always tinkering with their body.

Jim placed the signal jammer on Kit's arm. The silver ring fit perfectly over the blue circle. The cold underside made him wince when it made contact with his skin. Jim spun the top half of the jammer and it clicked into place, the bottom half magnetically stuck to Kit's skin due to the heavy metal strip embedded into his stamp. The jammer whirred and lights started to flash before the contraption produced a unique buzz then a beep and finally a chime. The jammer detached itself and Jim removed it revealing Kit's clean shoulder.

Kit marveled at his clean skin. "Holy shit," he whispered.

"You're damn right holy shit," Jim responded with a level of gravity that Kit rarely saw. "Now my turn." Jim did the same to himself with the jammer and moments later his blue stamp had disappeared. Tonight, they were not mucking around. Tai was covering up her indicator cross with make-up. Whilst the Jammer could remove the Blue Stamp as that was something mechanical and inserted as part of government law it could not remove the red cross which was a indicator produced by the bodies toxins.

"Fuck, I got the wrong blush," Tai cursed.

Jim looked over. "You're going to be all right?"

Tai shooed him off. "Yeah, yeah, I just need to use more of it."

Jim addressed the two of them like a mastermind before a bank heist. "All right, from what I know the jammer can only suppress our stamps for five hours before we have to re activate them again, so out by twelve or we turn into pumpkins, got it?"

The door handle rattled and all three shot back a look at the entrance. It rattled again, the door was locked but they could never be totally sure. It was too late to jump into the cubicles, so if someone was to break through, they would have been reported. The door knob rattled a few more times before finally it stopped and the sounds of footsteps faded away.

"Shit!" Tai breathed out.

All three of them looked back to the mirror and studied their new, clean skin form. They were speechless. Why were they becoming the thing they hated? Or maybe the clothes were secretly doing such a good job that deep down they were imagining what their life could have been, should have been, deserved to have been.

Jim hid the jammer under the counter with the sinks. "We'll come back here and I'll grab this later. If not me, one of you two."

"No going back now," Kit said.

Moments later, the trio were striding confidently over the campus grounds. There was a buzz in the air that only comes from being on a thriving university campus. They tried not to let the sheer beauty of the university overwhelm them, but it was impossible. They soaked in the history, the buildings, the architecture—an opportunity that they would never be afforded.

"Damn, it's another world, isn't it?" Jim said in a reverential, whispered tone.

Kit and Tai were speechless and could barely keep their mouths closed.

Jim shook off the spell and whispered again, "No, we got to pretend we belong here guys. No sight seeing, all right?"

The three of them shook it off and kept up the pace. Jim began playing with some velcro flap on his shoulder. He looked over; all three of them had the same flap on their clothes.

Tai looked over to Kit. "Psst, Kit, your watch."

Even though not as gaudy as everyone else's, it still looked incongruous compared to the rest of their attire. Ultimately, it was a dead give away and needed to go. He quickly shimmied it off and jammed it into his pocket revealing quite a large tan line where it usually sat.

Not long after, they reached the campus house hosting the party. Formed in blue stone over one hundred and fifty years ago with an imposing entrance of two large columns snaked in ivy. It was important, steeped in a history they would never know about and weirdly now wanted to know about. But all that mattered now was the party inside and whether they could get in.

The music and chatter coming from behind the walls made it seem like it was worth the risk.

Kit looked up at the line of students waiting to be scanned. "You know what, we should go separately. Just in case something happens, they can't associate us with each other."

Tai nodded. "Good idea."

Jim confidently skipped up the steps first. He wasn't nervous as he skipped up but was certainly shaking by the time he reached the top. A guard stood at the entrance holding a scanner. Each shoulder that passed him got scanned. Jim realized what the velcro patch was for now. He looked back at his friends and nodded to them whilst tapping the patch on his shoulder casually. Tai and Kit steadied themselves.

It was Jim's turn next. He stepped forward and opened his patch, the guard held the scanner on his shoulder for far too long. Finally, he pulled it back. Jim, Kit, Tai and the Guard waited for the reading to be spat out. Just when the guard was about to say something, a beep interrupted him, a good beep, the right sounding beep. The guard's face softened, and he nodded Jim through.

Tai smiled and went up next while Kit faded himself towards the back of the line to offer some distance. At the top of the stoop, Tai offered her shoulder, the same happened again. It was slow to process but, within minutes, she and eventually Kit joined Jim inside. The three of them kept their heads down and their faces neutral as they passed the entry threshold into the party house.

The three Rats-come-Clean Skins stood at the foot of the party, the most noticeable thing was that it wasn't much of a party. Yes, there were students, lots of them, and music, and booze, but something was missing. It was polite, and that reckless abandon that you associate with young adults partying was not there, replaced with something more controlled. There was life here; it just was another type—one they weren't used to.

Worse yet, everyone was built differently. They knew what the typical Clean Skin body type was but to see so many model thin girls and lithe boys in one place at the one time was unsettling. By comparison, Kit, Tai and Jim looked like pro athletes ready to plow through them like industrial farm equipment.

Tai was not impressed. "We wasted a jammer for this?"

Jim took stock of it all. "There is a party here, we just gotta find it… come on."

Tai grabbed Kit by the arm. "Come on, Kit, let's get fucked up."

* * *

On the other side of the party, outside, an illuminated pool was the centerpiece of the campus house. Chinese lanterns floated on top; again the same muted fun being had by the students. Josephine was standing with Elizabeth, who was every bit the spark of energy her video call projected her to be. One of the few overweight Clean Skins, Alexander, strolled up to the ladies. He carried his weight in a way that made him appear as thin as the others there.

Josephine felt non plussed by his presence. In fact she couldn't wait to leave.

Alexander kissed Elizabeth on the lips before settling back on Josephine. "I set you up with one of my gents and he tells me you left in the middle of the date."

Josephine scrunched her face. "Wait that was you?"

Alexander was shocked. "Of course, I knew you wouldn't listen to me so I got Elizabeth to set it up. You left him high and dry."

Josephine quipped back. "Well he left me bored and offended so I'd say we're even." She offered Alexander a polite and sarcastic smile.

"Last time I do that for you Josephine." Alexander sighed.

"Good. And it's Jo, not Josephine."

Alexander took a moments pause. "Not in our world

it's not. Maybe you should start living in it for once." He took Elizabeth by the hand and walked off.

Elizabeth looked back and offered a frustrated eye roll to her friend who was now alone at this party she didn't want to be at.

*   *   *

Across the pool emerged Kit, Tai and Jim. Jim had found a beer and Tai was eating some sort of food from a plate.

Jim made a face. "Urggh what is this shit?"

Tai spat out the food. "Yeah that's definitely fake meat," she huffed.

Kit had neither food nor drink and was scanning the party. He was bored and the novelty of sneaking into a Clean Skin party had worn off. He was ready to call it. He had nothing to gain from hanging around these people. He continued scanning the party lazily until he spotted someone across the pool.

For a second, he scanned right past the person before shooting back and clocking her. There she was, Josephine. His vision closed, everything in his periphery went black, like a pair of binoculars. It was just him and her even if she wasn't aware of it.

There was that shock of adrenaline that hit him in the chest, that excitement that made him want to jump the gun and miraculously walk over the water in the pool right toward her, but he knew better, especially at a party like this.

For a few seconds, nobody noticed until Jim looked at him and could see he had fallen in a state of comatose.

Kit kept his eyes on her and only moved his mouth "Shit, it's her."

Jim looked around but couldn't spot her. "Who?"

Kit nodded in her direction. "The girl from the youth group."

Jim followed Kit's eyes. "Holy shit it is her."

"Quick, hide behind that window before she sees you!" Jim let out a laugh.

Kit barely noticed. Something was stirring inside him. He was weighing up his life until now, concluding that life was, at the end of the day, made up of just a few moments. This was one of them. Something as simple as approaching her to talk might change his life in a way he could have never imagined. Everything in his life up until now had been the same, same people, same conversations, same fate waiting for him at the end. But tonight was different, his clothes, the party and now possibly the conversation he was going to have. It was time.

"Screw this." He began walking towards her. Whatever it was, it wasn't him. It was something else moving his legs. The excitement and courage had taken over.

Neither Tai nor Jim could believe it.

Jim called out, "She's not your type!"

"Says who?" Kit spat back.

"Society!" Jim answered, but it was too late.

Kit was crossing over to the other side. Deep down, Jim was afraid. What happened if Kit never came back?

Kit walked over, every step an attempt to psyche himself up. He could see her struggling to pour a beer from the keg. He figured this could be his way in. He calmly took a cup and waited behind her. "You need a hand?"

"I'm fine." Her voice was laced deep with frustration.

She turned around and was immediately hit with the mack truck that was Kit. He looked like a Clean Skin but something about the way he held himself made him magnetic. He looked sturdier, more capable than all these other boys. He looked like a man.

"Hey I'm Kit… Kitridge." He held out his hand.

Like the rest of him, it looked stronger than any of the hands on offer.

"Josephine… call me Jo." She gripped it, their shake lasting that moment longer than what would be socially acceptable for two complete strangers, it was naturally firm and left an impression on her.

Kit smiled. "Do you come to these…"

"Often?" She butted in. "Yes, too often."

"Lucky me, I may have caught you at your last one." Kit smiled back.

Josephine looked around, fed up with the people on display. "When you know what's on offer, it's hard to get excited."

"I'm on offer." His answer was so quick and confident yet earnest that it knocked her off guard.

Her response was fighting through her chuckle. "Ah okay, what are you offering?"

"Well for one, non invisible beer." He pointed to her empty plastic cup. "I saw your pretend pour before."

"Those things make no sense!" she arked back.

He took her cup and went over and primed the handle. "You see you have to pump it first." He poured her a beer as if he had whispered some magic words to the keg to make it obey him. He handed the cup back over. "Cheers." He held up his cup.

Josephine went to clink it.

He stopped her. "Nah it's gotta be like this, wrist to wrist because our cups are plastic."

"Why?"

"Because it's bad luck, and I wouldn't want to start this up on the wrong foot."

"Start what up?" she asked.

"Whatever this is going to be." He let the line linger before he took a sip.

She couldn't help but be intrigued by this guy.

Compared to her last date or even someone like Elizabeth's dude, Alexander, this guy in front of her had a weird reckless honesty that she had never witnessed before. His roguishness was undeniable and she had quickly found herself fighting the desire to learn more.

Usually she had a gift for seeing through bullshit but this guy either didn't have it or was better at hiding it than most. Ultimately, she couldn't place him and it was exciting her. "So what do you do here?"

Kit wasn't ready for that one. "Wow straight into it."

Josephine's interest waned immediately. "Well I know what that means…"

"What does that mean?" Kit felt amused.

"It means you don't have an answer." Josephine was definitely serious.

"I have an answer." He tried to keep the conversation light.

"Okay so what do you do?" She wanted to be proven wrong.

Kit wavered a bit. "Well, I'm a student of the world."

The answer was enough to send her walking in the opposite direction. "It was nice meeting you."

Kit couldn't believe it. In an instant, she had materialized into his life and, just as quickly, she had vaporized in a cloud of disillusionment.

Right at that second, a random yell came from across the pool and stopped everyone, like a record screech.

The entire party halted as a pair of security guards busted through the crowd trying to control a twisting and contorting woman. Kit's mouth dropped. It was Tai and she was making a scene. The guard from the entrance twisted her arm back and she let out the most painful of wails.

Most of the Clean Skins present had never seen brutality like this up close and it made them all uncomfortable. The other guard roughly steadied her arm and pulled out a contraption of his own and placed it on her shoulder. The piece of tech made a few beeps and revealed her blue ring. All the while the commotion had rubbed off her make up and revealed her red cross.

For a moment, the entire party froze. They didn't know what to feel. For a lot of them, this was the first time they had ever interacted or shared space with a Rat. Something about the visceral nature of the exchange, the raw human emotion on display, it hit a lot of these Clean Skins square in the heart.

Suddenly a blur flashed across both security guards. It was Jim as he landed a punch squarely on one of them, sending him to the floor. Kit had no choice. Under no accord of his own, his body went to rush the other guard but something yanked him back. He looked behind him. It was Josephine.

She had gotten hold of his jumper. "What the hell are you doing!"

He shot back at her. "Helping! Someone here has gotta be the difference!"

The sound of her own personal mantra being thrown right back in her face by this guy she had just brushed off was now all she could think about. "Let me handle this, they won't hit me." She stepped forward. "Let them go!"

The guard rolled his eyes as the other one had now captured Jim and tangled him in a headlock. "Hey, step back, they broke the law."

Josephine looked around. "Tell me, which law."

The guard had no time for this. "Listen I'm doing my job."

She couldn't believe it. "What? To be an arsehole. Do you know who I am?"

The guards had heard enough. Kit rushed in and held back Josephine who looked ready to climb on top of them. Subtly, Kit locked eyes with Tai.

Her look to him said it all: *Save yourself.*

The guards stiff armed Josephine out of the way as they rag dolled the couple back inside and out the front entrance. The entire crowd remained silent, the aftermath of what they just witnessed lasting only a few seconds before the music started again. Josephine looked to Kit, who was still holding her arm. She shoved him away still consumed by the injustice of what she had just witnessed. Storming inside, Kit watched her get swallowed up by the crowd. He rubbed his face. Now it was definitely over and time to go home.

The party had corrected itself. The incident was now a memory. Nobody was even remotely concerned about the fate of Tai and Jim. Kit sat on a stool alone and paralyzed. He didn't know what to do; more importantly, he didn't know why he hadn't gone home yet.

Maybe he held out hope that he and Josephine would cross paths again, or maybe he just wanted to remain amongst the vibe of it all, knowing that he'd never get the opportunity to be at a party like this again. He figured he'd might as well stay until he was told to leave. He played with his beer and swished the dregs of it around.

"Hey."

Kit looked up. It was Josephine, her face softer than before. He wanted to give her the brightest of smiles but kept it cool. "Oh hey." He matched her vibe.

"I'm sorry about before." Her tone was honest and a little bit tired.

He offered a warm smile in response. "Actually it was kind of impressive." He chuckled back.

"What, the lack of emotional control or the fact I said 'Do you know who I am?'" Her answer had them both laughing.

"I'm sure those two appreciate what you did."

Josephine dropped her shoulders. "I didn't do any-thing, actually nobody did. They just stood there. That's why I hate coming to these things. It's a bubble inside a bubble." She looked around, disgusted at her people.

Kit stood. "Yeah I think this might be my last one, too." He threw out a hand. "Well it was nice meeting you, Jo."

She shook it. Kit turned around and walked off. Jose-phine kept her eyes on him. Kit kept walking but as if sensing there was unfinished business, he turned around. There she was still staring at him.

The crowds, the music, the chatter, disappeared into the background. It was just them and nobody else.

He smiled at her and she smiled back, both of them relishing in this weird early courting dance they had randomly found themselves in. Somehow, in the space of an hour, they went from strangers to finding it impossible to turn away from each other.

A switch had accidentally been turned on and nei-ther wanted to turn it off.

CHAPTER 12
I'M HERE WITH YOU

The two of them walked the campus grounds. It was quiet, the sound of the party was now only a faint murmur in the distance. Random students walked and loitered on the manicured gardens but, for the most part, the campus felt like it was all theirs.

Josephine was listing the details of her degree. "Social Science, majoring in Sociology."

Kit nodded his head. "That explains the social conscience."

Josephine somewhat agreed. "It's also my duty."

This surprised him. "Your duty? What's your duty?"

"To raise awareness of Nox Anima. That's why we protest and host rallies and set up support groups and—"

"—start fights with security guards?" Kit interjected.

His quickness got her laughing.

"Someone from our side has to show them that we care. Plus it makes me feel better about all this." She motioned to the campus.

Kit followed her hands and looked around the campus with her. "You mean living and studying here?"

She nodded.

"Then give it up."

He was so nonchalant with his suggestion, none of this meant anything to him, it had no stakes and it was making him more attractive by the moment.

"What, University?"

"Yeah, make it your job. Show them you're legit. What have you got to lose?"

She had never been presented with that option and it was somewhat of a harsh truth. She took it as a slight against her commitment but was sort of turned on by him challenging her. She gave him the benefit of the doubt as he was too cute to start an argument this early in their flirting. "You think I'm going to bail after I graduate?"

"It's what Clean Skins do best. I mean *us*, we just coast right?" It was weird for Kit to use the word "us" but it also surprised him how easy it was to say it.

Josephine was defiant. "Well I'm different, I'm in it for the long haul, fully committed."

Kit nodded again, this time proudly. "That's good to hear." He stared at her for a moment, totally in love with her answer.

The silence between them allowed for the stuff left unsaid to be felt, a deep physical attraction that was beginning to brew. They continued to look at each other for a while, soaking in the other's traits. It was here they decided what they liked about each other.

Kit was getting lost in Josephine's eyes. There was an intensity to them, a depth he'd been searching for since Gem's death.

Josephine couldn't help but be drawn to Kit's build, and authenticity—again it was such a point of difference that she found herself sometimes losing focus on what he was saying. This annoyed her because it made her feel like some helpless damsel, which was not the case and definitely not the vibe she wanted to give off. She also sensed pretty quickly that this was not the vibe Kit was into either. If he was, he wouldn't be talking to her. So at times she would randomly find herself correcting or shaking off the spell of his shaved head or toned arms to refocus back on the genuineness of his words.

Josephine straightened herself once more. "So what are you committed to?"

"The moment…" His answer came with a self satisfied smile.

"Who's coasting now?"

Kit laughed. "Okay, yeah I have a job, I work for a clearance outfit. We go in and strip the apartments of those who had Nox Anima…"

This changed the tone of the conversation immediately.

"Oh that's like a job, *job*. You don't hear many Clean

Skins doing that type of work."

Kit panicked for a second, she was right, the job was synonymous with Rats and he quickly peddled for answers that would make his reasons for doing such work believable. "Yeah you don't, but it's not forever and it pays well. Look I don't have crowds cheering for me and sometimes there is the odd corpse but someone's gotta go in and respect the memories."

Now it was Josephine's turn to nod her head. "That's a nice way of seeing it."

"It's the only way of seeing it." His answer was propped up with a strong sense of pride and his own duty.

She sat with the answer for a while, and she felt a little jealous. This guy wasn't even trying and yet, she somehow felt like he was doing more for the Rat community than she ever could, but she quickly brushed it off as her inner competitiveness, something she had inherited from her father. "Is it true that before someone with Nox Anima dies they have a massive party? Like some sort of D Day celebration?"

Kit paused, the mention of the parties had caused him to think back on all the ones he had attended. There were a lot—acquaintances, close friends and even lovers. He cleared his throat. "Yeah, I've never been to one myself but yeah, I've heard they can get pretty loose. I imagine it's some hectic mix of a funeral and a wedding and a birthday all in one."

Josephine pictured the mash of those three pivotal life moments and gave off a weird smile before she looked back at Kit and thought to herself, *Who the hell is this man?*

The two eventually arrived at Josephine's college dorm. It was protected by a grand stone entrance and a wrought iron gate controlled by an electronic touch pad. The two of them hung around in that awkward post date loiter.

"Should we exchange profiles?" Josephine asked.

"I'm not on the cloud," Kit blankly responded.

Josephine got whiplash from his answer. A Clean Skin without a cloud was almost unheard of. "So where are you?"

"I'm here… with you."

His answer was both genuine, humble and border-line naïve. This man's ability to be in the present had left her speechless.

"…Ah okay, so how will you find me?"

He pulled out a smart phone.

Josephine started laughing. "Wait I gotta see this." She picked it off him and started inspecting it, "Is this real?" She studied it as if it was a relic dug out from the ground.

"Yeah it is. Does the same job as the cloud." Kit shrugged.

The phone pinged in her hand. "Oh you got a message

from Jim." She handed it back to him.

"56 2287 960, that's my number, you got that?" Kit said.

Josephine tapped her temple, signaling the cloud already had it. The two hung around for a few more beats.

"Well it was nice meeting you," Kit said before strolling away.

Josephine watched him walk away for the second time that night. "Hey, that thing you said at the party, about being the difference. What did you mean by that?"

Kit shrugged. "I don't know. I think my Nan said it." He turned around and kept walking. Looking down at his phone, he checked the message from Jim. *Need to post bail, grab the jammer, dirty cop, pigs.*

Josephine swiped her wrist on the gate and unlocked it.

In the bathroom, Kit reached under the counter where Jim had hidden the jammer. He pulled it out and pocketed it. While he took off his Clean Skin clothes, his shoulder stamp started blinking, like a failing fluro light. It blinked until finally it returned to full luminance again. He took a deep breath and looked at himself. A small smile came over his face, a sense of joy that had not been there for a long time, and it excited him.

*   *   *

Josephine lay in her bed, her bedroom a monument to her commitment to her cause. Rally posters of all the protests she had organized over the years looked down at her in a collection of proud life time achievements. While she looked up at her ceiling, the same smile came over her face that had come over Kit's. She had got this weird feeling; it felt like a longing, like a fear she had missed out.

Kit seemed so worldly, so self-aware and well-adjusted. She imagined the life he lived before he met her and how exciting it would have been—the parties, his cool friends, the experiences he would have had, the realness of it all. It made her feel sad that she was just meeting him now, that she had missed out on being with this guy and sharing in all those life occasions.

It scared her because she had never felt a pinging inside like this before. Maybe this was the feeling she didn't realize she needed, because maybe, just maybe, she had finally met a guy worth her time, someone she could grow with.

She reached over and turned off her bedside light.

CHAPTER 13
I THINK IT'S WEIRD

The next morning, Josephine and Elizabeth sat in a booth in the campus library. It wasn't really a booth. The booths had gone out with the books when the cloud was invented. Instead most kids sat on bean bags and studied their coursework off their cloud screens. Books were now kept behind bulletproof, Lucite glass in a temperature-controlled display room and restored and maintained by a curator. Libraries had now become museums dedicated to preserving knowledge. A book had not been written in twenty years, so the collection of books had now become big business, and every campus library was now worth millions. With every last edition of every book being the last, the older the university, the older the books the more valuable the collection.

Elizabeth scanned what appeared to be a student directory on her own cloud. Josephine grew tired, as if she had been watching her do this for hours.

"I told you he doesn't have a cloud."

Elizabeth leaned back, resigned. "I think it's weird."

"I think it's brave."

"I asked Alexander if he knew who he was and he said he had no idea. He looked through the party manifest from the night and there was no profile attached to his name, he said he could have been from our satellite campus." Elizabeth closed her cloud. "So how are you going to find him?"

Josephine shot up his phone number on her own cloud.

Elizabeth made a face. "What the hell is that?"

Josephine rolled her eyes. "It's his phone number."

"So he has an actual phone?"

"Yeah, like the rest of the world did thirty years ago."

"Well when it starts going from brave to weird, come find me," Elizabeth said before standing and stretching. As she walked past, she tapped behind Josephine's ear, and her cloud sucked back into her eye, disorienting her.

"Hey!" Josephine swatted at her.

Elizabeth let out a diabolical chuckle.

Josephine brought up his number one more time and studied it. It wasn't that Elizabeth was wrong, it was that Josephine didn't want her to be right. She wanted him to be the opposite of all things she had encountered and experienced with other guys over the years. She wasn't that experienced when it came to relationships. Her longest relationship had lasted eighteen months and that was just out of high school. He had dumped her when she started taking a real interest in Nox Anima and its impact on society. His exact words before he left were, "You used to be fun, Josephine, now you're just self righteous."

For a while she believed him, but the more she buried herself in the cause, the more she realized that they had simply outgrown each other. At that time, her father was happy they had split up. In fact, his words to her were the last ones she could remember that were truly fatherly, and she would always go back to them when a date had gone bad. "You are you, and fuck those who don't want to be on that journey." Ironically, it didn't seem like her father wanted to be on that journey with her anymore either.

* * *

The eastern sun streamed in through the window of Kit's apartment. It made the outside appear prettier than it actually was, just towers upon towers of the same-sized apartments with people dealing with the same life rate problem. How each of those people navigated Nox Anima was their own narrative, and as strong as a community the housing towers were they could be just as lonely too, because people deep down had their own story to deal with when time was of the essence.

Kit sat down, molding a lump of spinning clay, the brown water spilling over his hands, the metronomic noise of the creaky pottery wheel making that concussive sound every time it finished a rotation. Kit was focused on his creation, whatever it was going to be.

Nan sat next to him in her wheelchair. "Keep them steady, Ric."

Kit sent a quick glance up to Nan. "You're talking to Kit, Nan. Dad's dead. Remember?"

Nan shook it off. "Oh of course."

Kit's attention went back on his clay. He hadn't molded since Gem died but weirdly had a desire to make something today. He had a bunch of pent up energy from last night. It was good energy. Yet he needed an outlet for it. Seconds later, his phone vibrated. Kit didn't look up this time. "Nan, could you get that?"

She wheeled over, grabbed his phone, pulled up her glasses attached to her chain and leaned into the screen to read the message out loud. "If this is Kitridge…" Nan mouthed the name, "Kitridge."

Kit offered her a shrug.

Nan went back to reading the message on his phone. "I have a piano that needs moving." She looked back at Kit. "That sounds like a date." She raised an eyebrow.

Kit tried to suppress his smile but he was beaming from the inside out and it was impossible to ignore.

"So where are you going to take her?" Nan asked.

Kit shrugged. "Hopefully somewhere that accepts cash."

Kit banged his fist three times on the door before pulling away and making space for a moment of silence. He loitered around, the Clean Skin clothes from the party folded up in his hands. He was high up in the towers; behind him was a balcony railing and behind that were the sounds of the general melting pot of people that had created this overpopulated concrete community. The door swung open, revealing Jim with no shirt on. He nodded Kit inside.

As he walked through the apartment, it was evident that the way Jim spent his money and how Kit saved his directly related to how they grappled with the concept of the mutation. Whilst Kit had a goal—look after his Nan—Jim had his own. To buy everything he could because things made him happy. Needless to say, Jim was in the majority and Kit was in the minority.

Jim's place was styled to within an inch of its life. It resembled the interior of a nightclub crossed with a high-end retail street-wear store. His QLED screen was impossibly big and impossibly thin, the art on the walls was loud and bold, the couches deep with shallow backings made of black velvet. His circular coffee table was constructed of metal and glass, whilst skateboards lined one wall like an installation at a gallery.

Tai was under a blanket and appeared to be a shade greyer than she had been the other night. That rash of hers had made some serious headway up her arm and was now at her bicep. Jim looked back. "Mad thanks for the bail out the other night."

Kit waved it off, as Jim handed him the money to pay him back. "You keep it."

Jim scrunched his face. "What? Fuck you... no take it."

Kit took a moment. "Actually I was wondering if I could keep the jammer instead." His tone was conciliatory.

Jim knew the answer but asked anyway. "Why?"

Tai interjected. "Clean Skin chick, hey? Good for you."

Kit was trying to conceal his joy. Jim softened for a moment—how could he say no—but that feeling from the other night was rising again. His best friend was passing that invisible divide to the other side.

What would happen if she liked him back?

Worse yet what would happen if they fell in love?

Where would that leave him?

Jim had to say something as it was starting to get weird. "I hope she's worth it."

Kit shrugged. He hoped so, too. He looked over at Tai. "How you holding up?"

"Not great..." She coughed.

Jim looked back, tears brimming in his eyes. This was the beginning of the end, all three knew but none were going to verbalize it, let alone acknowledge it.

Kit wanted to say something but knew it would be pointless, the moment brought back memories of Gem, when they were a foursome and the idea of timing out and dying seemed so far away. When she died it took a long time for the three of them to find that joy as a trio, now it was being taken away again, just when they were finding their rhythm. It would have been easier if this death was caused by a person, at least there would be someone to hate together but instead this faceless killer was clearing the way for one obvious conclusion, these coming months would be their final moments of peace.

Jim lifted his head. "She's lying, handling it like a boss."

Tai smiled at Kit. "I think you may need those clothes for a little while longer."

Jim pointed to the Jammer. "One more date. You lose it, I'll kill you."

Kit didn't need to be told anymore. He was grateful and left knowing not to push his luck.

CHAPTER 14
WHAT IF I GET IT
WRONG?

Josephine picked at her health bowl, a combination of nuts, greens, tofu for protein, and other raw foods that looked more healthy than hearty. In fact nearly everyone in the restaurant was eating the same meal—everyone except Kit, who was hoeing into a steak.

Josephine watched him, a smirk over her face. "I'm surprised they had that on the menu." She chuckled.

Kit smiled through the chewing. The restaurant she chose was close to campus and popular with students. It was actually a regular cafe / diner but because everyone dressed in the way they dressed it looked far more high end than what the menu offered up. Still compared to the fast food dumps Kit was used to eating at this place was as good as a Michelin star eatery.

He looked around and paused for a moment. "How many of these dates are real?"

"What do you mean?"

Kit finished what was in his mouth. "I mean how many of these are cloud dates?"

Josephine smiled. "Oh yeah, well I guess any table you see that's empty but has that little black box in the middle, that's a cloud date."

Kit took a wider look around letting his imagination do the work. "You ever been on one?"

Josephine smirked. "Yeah, a few…"

"What are they like?" Kit was fully invested now.

Josephine pondered over it. "I mean they feel real if that's what you're asking, but you're never truly invested because you know if it turns to shit, you can always button off."

Kit scrunched his face. "Just like that?"

Josephine nodded. "Yeah, someone says something offensive or you can see it's going nowhere, you can just push the eject button."

Kit thought about it for a second. "So are you ever truly yourself, or you just a version of yourself that you hope doesn't get rejected?"

Now it was Josephine's turn to think deeply about the dating landscape. "Huh… Well I'm not going to leave you tonight."

"Well that's good, I was actually going to get you to pay for dinner."

Josephine could see the sarcasm and started laughing which got Kit smiling. She hadn't felt this comfortable or safe with a guy for such a long time.

Hours passed and empty desert bowls sat on the table. Both of them felt satisfied, the tone of the place had reached a late night relaxed level.

"So tell me, who made it your duty?" Kit asked.

Josephine was generally confused.

"The other night, remember, you said it was your duty. Raise awareness."

It took another moment but then it hit her. "Oh. Yeah. I come from a family of helpers. It's in the DNA. My father just happens to be Montgomery Dunn."

"Who?"

His answer stirred up a small level of insult within her, but the more she studied his face, the more she realized this guy had no obligation to know her family lineage. "Montgomery Dunn. He discovered Nox Anima, almost cured it."

Now it was Kit's turn to be blown away. "What? When was this, what was I doing?"

Josephine laughed. "Well, you were probably like five years old for one, by the time you were ten it was too late and the world had forgotten about him." Josephine quizzed. "So you're telling me you've never heard of him?"

"No, maybe, I can't remember, maybe I just forgot – what's he like?"

Josephine's tone dropped. "Depressed. Cynical.

Living in the past. Mostly because my mom and sister died."

Kit attempted to backtrack. "Oh, I'm sorry I didn't mean to—"

Josephine wasted no time and cut him off. "So are your parents happy with what you do?"

Kit was just as quick. "My parents are dead."

Josephine had no response.

"They died in a car crash when I was a kid."

Josephine looked down at her desert and swirled around the bits and pieces in her bowl. "Same here with my mom and sister. I don't remember much either."

A quiet beat fell between them, but it wasn't anything awkward, it was the opposite. It was comfort—comfort in knowing the other person understood something about them that very few people could, that the damage sudden loss did to someone at a young age was usually irreparable and at best suppressible. The moment produced a smile that bounced between them and grew wider and wider by the second.

"You think now's a good time to ask for a kiss?" Kit chuckled.

Josephine burst out laughing, the noise so loud and sharp she had to cover her mouth.

Kit waved it off as if to say: *I'm just kidding.* Her laughter petered out and Kit sat back and relaxed. "So what would you do if they cured Nox Anima? I mean, what else have you got in the deck?"

It wasn't something that she thought about much, maybe because it defined her. It was hard to think of who she was without the mutation. "You know the truth? This sounds terrible but part of me doesn't want them to find a cure."

Kit was smart enough to know this answer meant more than what it sounded like at first blush. "Really?"

Josephine immediately back peddled. "I don't mean it like that… But without Nox Anima, what am I? Just another Clean Skin with ninety-five years of life and no idea how to contribute. What if I get it wrong?"

Kit looked her in the eye and told her without hesitation, "Maybe you have ninety-five years to get it right?"

His response was so quick, so incisive, so mature yet so simple that it almost broke Josephine's brain. How did a Clean Skin grow up to be so well adjusted and so full of wisdom yet humble to the point of no ego? Whatever it was, this guy was a gem, a total rarity in her world.

Whilst for Kit, it was impossible not to admire this woman's guts, guile and integrity, she didn't have to stick her neck out for anyone, but here she was getting down in the trenches with his folk and wanting nothing in return other than to see them get treated like equals. She was an anomaly, it was as simple as that.

Outside, they walked side by side. It was that close

proximity where both wanted to hold hands but neither was game to make the first move so they rubbed shoulders instead knowing it would happen organically. The restaurant was still buzzing behind them, the pavement was wet and glistening from the street lights.

Kit looked behind him.

"Why you keep looking back?"

He waved it off. "Ah nothing."

She scanned around for his car. "So where is your ride?"

He pointed to a push bike chained to a bar.

She kept searching. "Where?"

He pointed again. "There."

She did a double take. "A bike? Wow you really like doing things the hard way, don't you?"

He cooly shrugged it off. "Maybe I like doing things the real way."

*   *   *

Back at the restaurant, a waiter thumbed through the cash left by Kit.

Another waiter walked by and spotted the currency. "Is that cash?"

"Yeah, he just left it and scurried out" The waiter rushed to the window just in time to clock Kit on his bike.

Kit glanced back and the two of them locked eyes for a second, both knowing they would never see each other again. He kicked the bike into gear and peddled away with Josephine sitting on the back with her arms around him.

The waiter turned away from the window and looked to the other waiter. "The boss is going to kill us."

Josephine gripped Kit's chest. His toned arms and ripped torso turned her on. She wasn't used to his physicality, watching his muscles work and move and do it with ease turned something on inside her that was primal. It felt exciting because it was new. There was something capable about Kit's body and it made her feel like he could handle her alpha energy, or maybe he was just a direct reaction to all the other guys she dated. Or at least been set up with. Or, possibly, for the first time, she had simply found her equal.

The bike skidded over the puddles as the low sun reflected orange and pink light into their faces.

Kit looked back at her. "Stand up on the pegs."

Josephine awkwardly hoisted herself onto her feet, her hands on his shoulders. The last time she had been on a bike was as a child playing with her twin sister. It brought back a flood of memories she wasn't quite ready for; she kept her hands on his shoulders, she wasn't ready to let go.

"Okay now close your eyes."

She closed her eyes.

Kit gritted his teeth and stepped up his cadence, his legs turning over double time. The wind blew through her hair and kissed her face, then something happened, something automatic. Slowly, she lifted her arms, holding them out like a plane. She let the wind embrace her. The weight of trying to rally crowds, organize protests and look after her father all melted away. An image of her and her sister playing on their bikes flashed before her eyes. For just that second, she was floating amidst a sea of nothingness and nostalgia. For the first time ever in her life, she let go.

Kit and the bike came to a graceful stop in the middle of the university campus. "Well here you are."

Josephine stepped off and walked over to the handle bars. Kit slumped over them catching his breath. Josephine touched his face. He was glistening with sweat, again that physicality so foreign to her but so erotic.

"You're hot."

Kit took a deep breath. "So are you."

They stared at each other.

"So what are you looking for?" Josephine asked.

Kit thought about it for a second. "In what?"

"In a person." Josephine's response was unwavering, the last few hours with this guy had her imagining scenarios with him years into the future and she wasn't afraid to show it.

Kit thought about it some more. "Why don't we say it at the same time."

Josephine loved the idea. The two of them looked at each other, no words needed, they both liked each other equally and both knew it, it made her blush.

"Okay. On the count of three…" She chuckled.

"Okay. One, two, three—"

Josephine blurted. "—Authenticity."

Kit spat out. "—Time."

Their words merged and mushed into one mangled mess. Slowly, they leaned into each other, they hovered for a moment, then finally, they kissed. It was slow at first, each feeling the other out. Kit untangled himself from the bike to get closer as it fell to the ground with a clang. Quickly it escalated. Kit gently put his hand on her chin and opened her mouth deftly as he kissed her. His other hand went around the small of her back and brought her in close. He had locked her in, his stiffness pressed against her vulva was signaling his intentions.

The pressure down there got her excited, it brought about something animalistic in her as she ramped up the momentum of the kissing and aggressively shot her tongue down his mouth. As if reading her mind, he begun sucking it and it was there she felt sensations she had not felt in years, she was melting in his arms which held her tight and close and made her lose sense of who she was.

Finally they both pulled apart, all they could think about was kissing again.

Josephine looked up at him. "You want to come back to mine?"

Kit nodded, and they kissed again. For a moment, Josephine was out of her body, looking down at herself, making out with Kit. She realized it had been a long time since she had kissed anyone.

CHAPTER 15
FINAL APPROACH

Josephine's dorm room was quiet. It was the middle of the night. The only noise was the slight hum of the campus and distant city traffic. Josephine was asleep in a post coital haze. She looked happy but also appeared dead to the world. Kit slowly rose from the other side of the bed and crept to the bathroom. A soft yellow light clicked on and bathed her face partially but was not enough to wake her.

In the bathroom, Kit looked at himself, his shirt off, his shoulder clean. He looked back at Josephine, peaceful in her slumber, then to himself. "When am I going to tell her?" He rubbed his temples hoping to come up with some easy answer but nothing came.

The stamp on his shoulder began to flicker, instantly he started to sweat. Kit tapped his shoulder as if it was a TV giving off static. "Don't do this to me." He kept tapping as if that was going to make a difference. His stamp flickered some more before finally disappearing again and leaving a clean shoulder. Kit sucked in a huge cloud of air in relief not realizing he had held his breath the entire time his stamp was malfunctioning. He breathed in again, how long had he not been breathing for? Resting himself up on the bathroom vanity, he wondered how long before his Stamp would reappear and he would have to use the signal jammer again. "What the hell are you doing man?" He took a moment to settle his nerves. He left the bathroom, clicked off the light, and got himself back into bed.

Josephine was still asleep but sensed his presence. She leaned over and threw an arm around him and got in close. Kit remained wide eyed, looking at the ceiling.

It was morning and orange light bathed the dorm room. Morning foot traffic and student chatter emerged outside. This time, it was Kit's turn to be dead to the world. Then, out of nowhere a noise, something similar to a jet engine, roared and filled the entire space. Kit shook himself awake. Startled, the first thing he did was check his shoulder, still clean. He breathed in. He was okay. Then he looked over and there was Josephine, her cloud screen projecting out what looked like an airport runway.

"Is that an airplane?" Kit had no idea what was going on.

Josephine was focused and using her hands to direct airport traffic. "Yeah it's called Final Approach. You get to be an air traffic controller. Sorry I could only watch you sleep for so long before it started feeling creepy"

Kit smiled "Watch as long as you want"

A sleek, subsonic Concord was gently taken in for landing. Josephine's hands cut the air like an orchestra conductor. "QF four-five-four taxi across the twenty-eight-L, then contact ground one twenty-one point eight zero. Welcome to San Francisco."

Kit shook his head. "You Clean Skins," he muttered. The minute the phrase left his mouth, Kit froze.

Josephine looked over to him. "What?"

Kit took a moment to realize she hadn't heard him. "Ah nothing." He got out of bed quickly before another brain fade occurred, and he chucked on a t-shirt and his jeans. Looking around, he took careful notice of all the protest posters plastered on the wall—each one loud, and aggressive and designed to whack you over the head with a message.

March for making Nox Anima a Memory.

Kit leaned in. "So these are the things you organize?"

Josephine glanced over. "Yeah that was my first."

Kit slowly paced around the room taking in each one. "So where do you host them?"

"On Campus. You should come."

He nodded. "You should do them outside campus. In the world. Where the real people can see it." He stopped at a photo frame, and picked it up. It was Josephine and her youth group. "These the kids you help out?"

She nodded.

"Where they from?"

"The Flats." The incessant questions were starting to wear her down but she also found the humor in his curiosity.

"You been there before?" he asked.

She finally paused her game and sent a big tired sigh his way. "You gonna ask me about every bit of crap in my room or you going to help me land some planes?"

Kit smiled and got back into bed with her. "Okay, sub me in!" He started waving his hands. "Pause, un pause, land the plane."

Her screen didn't respond, a plane sat there idling on the tarmac. Josephine cackled.

"What's wrong with your plane?" Kit joked knowing full well he had no idea what he was doing.

Josephine looked him in the eyes, he didn't have a cloud so he couldn't play the game. She grabbed his arms gently and lowered them "You need a cloud to play." She could see the disappointment in his eyes, another chance lost to be fully part of her world.

Both remained silent and just sat in the space of each other's bodies. Her knee now on top of his, his hand resting on her leg. Neither wanted to destroy the moment with words, both knew what the other was feeling so it didn't matter what the other was thinking. They leant in again and kissed, it was as electric as the night before. Quickly it evolved, hands groped all the areas that turned them on, Josephine went to take his shirt off, but he stopped her and instead instigated the same on her. She didn't think much of it in the thick of the sweat and the sex and so just let the sensations carry her back to the place where she felt like she was finally winning life on all fronts.

Yet amidst all this Kit kept one eye open, as if pleading with Nox Anima to leave them alone for this moment, it was theirs, and if he could just enjoy these fourteen hours without the spectre of his mutation rearing its head then he would pay it back by revealing everything to Josephine. But for now he was just a guy, wanting to be left alone, so he could fall in love in peace.

* * *

Josephine arrived again at her father's place, ready to help him clear out his study. The self driving car came to an elegant stop and she stepped out. She smiled. The residual intimacy she had enjoyed over the last fourteen hours was still vibrating through her body. She had so much of it that she wanted to share it with anyone she made contact with. She entered the house, hoping that her joy would infect her father.

Montgomery's study was a mess—stacks of books, five feet high, folders strewn all over the ground—making it impossible to walk without sliding on some piece of paper or important document. The room was Montgomery's sanctuary and an insight into who the man used to be, a lifelong battle into first understanding Nox Anima and then trying to beat it.

Half an hour later Josephine found herself knee-deep in paperwork, scanning folders, looking at books, trying in vain to create some sort of system. She found a stack of prescription pads, she noticed a few of them scribbled with the names of some medication, mostly anti-depressants. She took a second to look at her father, for a moment she empathized with him as he stood there in his crumpled posture staring at two whiteboards. Equations scrawled over them in a fashion that screamed both genius and borderline unstable. Coincidently, it was similar in style to those Josephine made when prepping speeches.

"So many wasted nights." There was a deep resignation in his voice.

Josephine looked up at him from the floor. "You want these?" She held up a few books.

It took a moment for Montgomery to shake out of his self-pity but he finally looked back. "Ah… bin them, bin it all."

A few hours later, the room was in some sort of order. Ultimately, only two piles remained, keep and throw away—most, if not all, the paperwork and books were tossed in the throwaway pile. It looked like the precursor to a book burning ceremony, one where a violent regime was hell bent on destroying all knowledge.

Josephine wheeled over something that was living under a tarp. Montgomery stood there, something was on his mind. Josephine pulled off the tarp and stuffed it under her arm, waving away the dust and getting hit by a few coughs. Underneath stood a beige machine the size of a small filing cabinet.

Josephine ran her hand over the smooth surface. The thing looked like it was stolen from a hospital. "Is this the Nox Anima box?"

Montgomery took a moment. He could barely look at the thing. That box had betrayed his trust. "Yeah. It was."

Josephine knelt down and studied it. "We learned about this my first year in college. Still don't know why this thing isn't in a museum."

Montgomery let out a small *pftt*. "That's because it didn't do what I promised it would."

Josephine was not convinced. She studied it further, looking at all sides. Maybe this thing would talk to her. "Maybe it just needs a tweak. Maybe the answer is still in there?"

Montgomery had had enough. "You know what, wheel it out, we don't need it."

Josephine stood up. "Are you nuts? Mum would have made you keep it."

"Yeah, well, she was the positive one."

Both lamented her absence.

"Is it wrong I don't remember the accident?" she asked.

"No you were too young, and thankfully not in the car." Montgomery put his hand on Josephine's shoulder. It didn't go unnoticed, the memory of his wife made him take stock of what he still had.

"Do you ever think about the person who killed them?"

Montgomery closed his eyes. Whoever that person was, he was picturing them right now. "Every single day." Montgomery breathed in deep. Tears had stopped forming years ago but the pain was still there.

Josephine stood still. "When did you know she was the one?"

Montgomery softened a little bit. He may have been gradually estranging himself from his daughter but he could still tell when one of her questions was more than just a question. "The day she died, because I knew then, there was no way I could ever replace her. Take it to the garage, we'll keep it there." He left Josephine alone with the machine as if to say, *It's your problem now.*

CHAPTER 16
I'M A VAMPIRE

Anytime the weather was good, the Rats were out. The day was cool and sunny and the towers were as much a place to live as they were a place to socialize. Underneath each tower were the open parking bays. Most of the cars parked underneath looked similar to Jim's. Mustangs, Dodge Chargers, Skylines, anything that could be souped up, pimped out, tricked up. Jim was replacing one of the lights while Kit sat on the flat bed scrolling through his phone, researching Clean Skin fashion trends.

"Tell Tai thanks. I think this girl was starting to wonder why I kept wearing the same shit every time we met."

Jim didn't seem to notice the comment. Instead, he answered matter of factly, "Did you bring the jammer?"

Kit didn't respond, Jim stopped. He knew immediately what that meant. Standing up from the light, he dusted his hands. His stare was enough to force Kit to justify himself.

"I just need it a little longer, man." The answer made

Kit feel like he was breaking the unspoken code of the Flats, but in truth he was quickly becoming a flakey friend.

"You know your stamp is gonna stop responding to that thing soon. Then what you gonna do?"

Kit shrugged. He didn't want to think that far ahead because he knew the outcome was going to be a shit-storm. Ironically, if a Rat was ever going to have to consider the future, this would be the time.

Jim was none too impressed with his nonchalant shrug. "I don't know if you've noticed but our little trio ain't gonna be around for much longer. When Tai goes, I got no one left."

Kit was immediately taken back by the comment. "You got me!"

"Do I? Doesn't look like it. Remember when Gem died? Now I need you here for me and Tai, so please, bring me the jammer so I can take my girl to a nice dinner one last time, okay? I didn't get that thing so her and I could eat Rat food for the fiftieth time."

Kit nodded. He didn't need any more prodding, he knew Jim was right. A silence fell between the two as Jim went back to fixing the headlight. Kit mulled around for a moment. There was something else he wanted to ask, but after that conversation, he wasn't so sure. But he decided to ask anyway. "Actually I need one other thing."

Jim wanted to smack his best friend upside the head but he suppressed his annoyance. "What?" he asked sharply.

Kit was already apologetic. "I need the truck."

*   *   *

That night the sky was clear and looked like a black canopy with glowing holes punched through it. Jim's truck stood parked in the middle of a barren field. On one side, a two meter tall chain link fence topped with barb wire stretched as far as the eye could see. On the other side, red and blue lights blinked on and off in a timed formation, whilst others ran alongside the ground edging out a wide stretch of tarmac. Josephine stood on the back of the trailer, looking back at Kit who was sitting down. He had a wry smile on his face.

Josephine felt like he was hiding something. She kept looking around. "What am I doing up here?"

Kit smiled even wider but gave her nothing. She shook her head before pausing. She heard a slight rumble. She froze. Kit couldn't help but laugh to himself watching her trying to piece it all together.

Out of nowhere, a thunderous roar blanketed them. Josephine shot her head upright just in time to watch the underside of an Airbus A380 scream overhead. She let out a scoff, in disbelief. The plane landed in the distance, the screech of its wheels scorching on contact with the bitumen and echoing through the barren airfield. The two of them sat in the silence enjoying the moment.

"It's a real life Final Approach." Kit cupped his hands.

"LH three twenty-three taxi across the fourteen D, then contact ground one thirty-one point nine zero. Welcome to Paris." Josephine turned around. Revealing the biggest smile, she held out a hand. "Here let me show you."

Kit leaped up and gave her his hand. She positioned him in front of her and held his hands like a puppet master. The two of them waited. It was silent, nothing needed to be said, whatever this moment was both knew they didn't want it to end. Suddenly, the familiar rumbling returned. It grew until it was deafening. Both looked up as Josephine waved Kit's arms around as if he was directing the plane and its landing gear. The plane hit the tarmac and Josephine lowered Kit's arms.

"Congratulations, Kit, you just safely landed eight hundred fifty-three souls." She let go of Kit's arms and stood by his side. "You ever traveled before?"

Kit shook his head. "No, but I got a place in mind when I do."

"Where?"

"Tropea, it's in Italy, in the deep South."

Josephine turned to face him, but his attention was taken by a distant police siren. He tensed up as if readying himself to make a getaway. Gradually, the siren faded and Kit dropped his shoulders. It didn't go unnoticed by Josephine.

"Sorry what?" Kit said coming back to the moment.

Josephine was bemused by his vague out. "Tropea, why there?"

Kit slowly shook his head. "I don't know, I just know part of me belongs there. What about you?"

Josephine let out a big sigh—filled with regret. "I've been meaning too, but I don't know. I'm scared to go on holidays. I figure I'll lose my edge, lose my hunger."

Kit nodded in understanding. "I guess it depends what you value, maybe you'll lose some edge but gain some perspective." He backtracked. "Not saying you don't have any, but I figure there is so much for us to learn outside of our bubbles."

*　*　*

It was morning but still dark. That moment before the sun rose. From inside, condensation had accumulated on the windows. Kit was asleep, Josephine was awake, leaning on her side. She had been watching Kit for a while. Something about him and the way he slept calmed her nervous system when she hugged him. She ran her fingers through his hair.

He stirred awake. It took him a moment to remember they spent the night in the truck. "You been watching me sleep?"

She smiled softly. Suddenly, blurry red and blue lights blanketed them as they shielded their eyes. It was accompanied by a whoop.

Josephine sat up. "What the…?"

Kit remained lying down, he knew exactly what this was. Josephine quickly put her clothes on and so did Kit. The sound of law enforcement boots crunching gravel moved closer and closer until it concluded with a light tap on the window of the truck.

"I'm gonna need you two to step out of the car."

Josephine looked at Kit. She could see he was freaking out. "Kit, what's wrong, we haven't done anything illegal?"

He nodded silently but couldn't shake the fear. "Miss."

Josephine stepped out followed by Kit. The sun had risen quickly in the meantime.

The policeman stood firm—his attire pressed clean and crisp, perfectly assembled for maximum intimidation. He looked past Josephine. He could spot a legitimate Clean Skin from a mile away so he focused solely on Kit. "You, I need you over here."

Kit marched over, his stride had that heaviness to it, as if he was walking to his own execution.

"Please take off your shirt."

Josephine couldn't believe it. "He's a Clean Skin, like me."

The policeman was confident. "You sure about that? Take your shirt off now." His tone sliced through Josephine's high pitched pleading.

Kit paused, in turn, it made Josephine question him.

"Now" the policeman yelled.

Kit gritted his teeth and took off his shirt revealing a clean shoulder and vindication for Josephine.

"You see!"

The policeman stood there calculating his next move.

"Where's your cloud?"

Josephine yelled back. "Not all of us have clouds asshole."

The policeman shot back at her with a glare. "You… in the car."

Josephine leaned forward. "Make me."

"Okay, you want to be out here for this?"

The policeman had a surety to him that was making Josephine uneasy, as if he was holding a set of aces. He reached into his back pocket, and pulled out a scanner, but it didn't look like the one that was used at the party. This one looked different—big, heavier, more high tech, the type issued for law enforcement only.

He grabbed Kit's arm and slammed him face first into the bonnet of the truck. "You haven't seen one of these before, I bet." He threw her the biggest of shit eating grins as he ran his police issue scanner over Kit's shoulder. "You ready for this sweetie?"

The scanner made a bunch of noises, all of them ominous, before pulsing out a sound that could only be described as alarming. The policeman removed the scanner and revealed Kit's blue subdermal ring. There it was. It had frozen her feet to the ground.

The policeman yanked Kit up by the neck. "You are under arrest for the intentional hiding of your status as a carrier of Nox Anima, intention to deceive a Clean Skin citizen with your status and illegally engaging in a relationship with a Clean Skin citizen."

Kit shot up breathless and looked around. He didn't know where he was and it took him a good fifteen seconds to realize he was in Jim's truck and that he'd been dreaming. Josephine kept calling his name, but he was still struggling to shake the terror from the nightmare he just had.

Josephine grabbed his hands and turned his head her way. "Kit, it's okay, you were just having a dream."

Kit's chest rose up and and down but was finally slowing as was his heart rate. "Did I say anything whilst I was dreaming?"

"No."

He let out a final big exhale and closed his eyes. "I'm okay."

"Well that's good," Josephine said. "I actually wanted to ask you something."

Kit nodded, he had finally settled down enough to be present again. "Yeah give me a minute." The two of them sat quietly whilst he composed himself. "Okay, I'm good now."

"You sure?" Josephine looked him in the eye. She had never seen anyone so physically affected by a dream.

He nodded back, that stillness was back. "Yeah, what is it?"

Josephine took a second. "I've been thinking… I want you to meet my father."

This made Kit sit up. "All right. Let's do it."

His response was genuine, Josephine couldn't contain her excitement. "Great, and maybe I can see where you live?"

Kit responded quickly but not truly, "Sure we can do that."

Josephine picked up on it. "I don't care where you live."

Kit knew she wouldn't, but that wasn't the problem. "Yeah I know."

She placed a hand on him, wanting Kit to know she was the real deal. "Actually there is something else."

Kit paid attention. "What's that?"

Josephine took a deep breath. "I'm a Vampire."

"You're telling me this now!"

She flipped onto her back, lying flat again. "I think you're ready for it, okay, so this is how a Vampire wakes up in the morning… or night." She crossed her arms over her chest and looked over at him, a smile across her face. "You ready to live forever?"

Kit nodded.

"Okay pull that lever."

Kit pulled the chair's lever and the seat smoothly adjusted itself upright, bringing Josephine with it. She made a creaking noise and coupled with her arms crossed and the magical way in which she assumed the seated position, the whole move made her look like Dracula.

Kit started cackling. "What the hell was that sound?"

Josephine laughed back. "That was the coffin opening! Okay put me back to sleep."

He was still laughing as he pulled back on the lever and sent the seat back into the recline position. She made the same sound again forcing them both into hysterics. Seeing her comfortable enough to try and make him laugh for the first time filled him with all sorts of excited feelings about their future, she had revealed another layer and he was all in.

CHAPTER 17
RECESSION RESISTANT

Kit sat in the back seat with Josephine. Her family's self driving car whizzed them through the pristine neighborhood her father lived in and anyone else that occupied the one percent of the one percent.

Josephine noticed Kit was gripping the passenger side handle. "You'll be fine, my father's cool… sometimes."

Kit shook his head. "No, I've just never been in a car that drives itself."

Josephine chuckled and threw her hands up. "Look no hands."

Kit couldn't shake the nerves. He tried to occupy himself with the disparity on display out the window. It worked. University was one thing, at least people there cared, or pretended to, but here, people didn't, or maybe they couldn't, because whatever this was, it remained unburdened by what was happening out there.

The car came to an elegant stop. Kit got out and his eyes were immediately drawn to Josephine's family home. Everything that Josephine had gotten used to was a detail Kit found fascinating—the peeling paint, the chipped windows, the overall feeling of neglect. It surprised him. It made Josephine seem even more down to earth.

She walked past him. "I think houses look like their owners after a while."

Kit screwed his face, not knowing what that meant or what to expect inside. She waved him in.

Inside the main entrance, Kit locked eyes with the family portrait. Josephine on the other hand was looking down the hallway. There was a light and some familiar sounds. Her heart sank. It had been the first time in a long time since she had brought a guy home and he was going to see her father in one of his memory bot funks talking to her dead mother and twin sister.

Kit looked over. "I didn't know you were a twin."

Josephine's attention was on what her father was doing. Then she glanced over. "Yeah, that was the sister who died. Come on, let's meet my dad." She was none too thrilled.

As they walked down the hall and rounded the corner, they entered the kitchen. Josephine let out a huge sigh, a look of relief mixed in with some pride washed over her. There was Montgomery—clean shaven, music playing, standing upright, and cooking dinner. Josephine felt ashamed she had not given him the benefit of the doubt. The man could flick it on when he needed to. It had just been that long she figured the switch had been rusted shut.

"Hey, Dad."

Montgomery looked up, smiles and bright eyes. "Hey honey. And you must be Kitridge." Montgomery wiped his hands on his kitchen apron and shook Kit's hand firmly.

"Pleasure to meet you, sir."

He waved it off. "Call me Monty. What have you got there?"

Kit presented a bottle of wine.

"Crack it open, let's have a glass." He threw his daughter a look as if to say: *See, your old man has still got it.*

Kit looked around; he watched the two robotic arms behind the glass make dinner. It was mesmerizing. Again, something he had only ever heard about in whispers. "Ah… where is your bathroom?"

Montgomery responded instantly. "Upstairs, third on your right."

Upstairs in the bathroom Kit splashed water on his face. Tilting open the medicine cabinet, he started perusing what was behind the mirror. It was a force of habit. Rats were always smashing all types of pharmaceuticals. It was how you got to know someone, know the drugs, know the personality. Although, this time, Kit was learning a lot more about who Montgomery *used* to be. He figured maybe this stuff was old and he hadn't bothered to chuck it out. Nevertheless, he found a collection of prescription bottles that covered the gamut of someone suffering from a lot of everything—pills for depression, sleeping, anxiety, calming. Kit took a few of the calming ones and then poured out a bunch of the others and put them into his pockets.

Taking off his shirt, he pulled out the jammer from his pocket and placed it over his ring. Automatically, it set itself into motion—the familiar click, clack, whizz and whir followed before the final beep. Kit lifted it off but his ring remained. What the hell?

Suddenly, the ring flickered, then flickered faster before finally disappearing. Kit remembered to breathe again because he had forgotten in those few moments. Slipping on his t-shirt, he took one of those long, reflective looks at himself and once again asked, "How long can you keep this up?"

When he walked down the hallway, he found a random door open just enough to entice him to take a peek inside. Peering through, he deftly pushed it open with his finger and walked through. Inside, he caught a glimpse of what Josephine, and her father were attempting to tidy the other day, but in effect, it was still in a state of shambles. Kit took a step inside and took it all in.

"Find the bathroom okay?"

The voice made him freeze. It was Josephine thankfully—who knew how awkward it would have been if it was her father.

Kit turned around. "Yeah, thanks."

Josephine nodded him downstairs. "Dinner is ready."

Dinner had been eaten. Dirty plates sat on the table along with empty bottles of wine. The three of them were laughing as Montgomery finished an embarrassing story about Josephine when she was young. She just sat there shaking her head, wishing the whole thing was over but was also being a good sport about it. Finally, Montgomery finished up, leaving the three of them to sit in silence and lament at times gone by.

Montgomery's gaze lingered as he caught sight of something. Immediately he sobered up. It was the tan line that sat on Kit's wrist which peeked ever so slightly out from his sleeve, but to someone as wise as Montgomery, it was unmistakable. He cleared his throat and leveled his gaze at Kit. The laughter seemed like a world away now. Kit noticed this and offered a polite smile back, hoping his gaze would soften… it didn't.

"So, Kit, you go to the gym?"

Josephine scrunched her face. The question was odd.

Kit thought nothing of it. "Ah yeah, I do."

Montgomery nodded as if he already knew the answer. "Any reason?"

Josephine butted in. "Dad, what are you on about?"

"I'm just curious, it's not something our people do."

Kit kept it cool. "I guess it's a social thing."

Montgomery kept his gaze. "Keeping fit, yeah that's important."

Another awkward pause followed.

"Out of interest Kitridge, who did you vote for in the last election?"

Now Josephine was pissed. "Dad, are you serious?"

Montgomery shrugged. "He doesn't have to answer it."

Kit interjected. "Pickering."

His answer silenced the table.

"I voted for Pickering."

Now Josephine wanted answers. "You voted for a candidate with Nox Anima?"

Montgomery casually quipped, "Well I would hardly call him a candidate. He wasn't affiliated with any legitimate party. I would say he was more of a novelty, a token"

Kit turned to her. "I voted for the most honest candidate out there."

"You think that was wise? Giving power to someone who won't be around to face the consequences of their actions?" Montgomery's tone was borderline parental now.

Kit paused for a moment. "I thought about it for a while... I get it, it was a risk, but the fact he somehow made it onto the ticket was such a big deal, even if it was all for show. If you ask me, he was the only person who understood how it worked from both sides."

Montgomery started chuckling. "I would like to think I have a pretty good handle of both sides."

Kit didn't disagree. "I'm sure you do but in all your time did you ever separate the mutation from the person?"

Montgomery was about to answer back but looked at his daughter and thought better of it.

Kit kept going. "Let's say a young woman with Nox Anima earns herself a wad of cash dancing at the club. She takes that money, goes to the pawn shop and buys herself a nice big flat-screen TV. Now, on the other side of the country, the same thing is happening, except it's a guy, and he's just finished a shift in a scrap yard, and he's bought himself a shiny second-hand necklace with his wad of cash. You... Me, we all go about this life like it's never going to end. Education, travel, expanding credit cloud debt, it's all propped up by one thing, a cash economy that we'll never see, use or touch. And it's the *single reason* our world is now recession resistant." Kit let that sit for a moment before ending with his closing argument. "We're only *half* of the equation. So how on earth do you justify voting for only half a candidate?"

The smile on Josephine's face was a combination of utter pride for her man and a big f— you to her father and she made sure both could see it in equal measure. Montgomery was rendered speechless by the response; usually, he would throw some science and statistics as a rebuttal, but they seemed pointless because it would make him seem out of touch.

Kit's response was a real-world response so Montgomery just lifted his hands as if to say, *How can I argue with that.*

Finally, it was time to go home. It was late. The houses twinkled under the night sky, which was full of stars—another added bonus of not having to live and compete with the bright lights of the city. Josephine hugged her dad as Kit stood there watching the two of them.

"Bye, Dad, thanks for dinner."

Montgomery's hug was different. His eyes were open. He knew what his daughter didn't but knew he had to let her find it out for herself. He offered a smile back but could only produce half of one. Josephine stepped into the car. Kit looked up at Montgomery whose gaze was unwavering.

"Until next time, Kit."

Kit dropped his keys in response to his Rat name. He crouched down and picked them up, his hand trembling. He stood back up, pretending the jab had no effect and shot back a smile. "Until then."

As the car drove off, Montgomery walked out onto his driveway and watched them disappear down the boulevard.

The next day, Kit stood by his promise and escorted Josephine into the Flats to see his side of town. Holding her hand, he led her through the towers, except the towers looked different. They were grey not brown like the ones where Kit lived. The activity was the same, the people were the same but it felt different, like a different flavor and it made Kit walk around with an air of caution.

"So this is where you live?" she asked.

Kit looked back at her. "Not exactly, my area is swarming with police right now, but it's basically the same as this, different tower same shit.

"And you choose to live here?"

He shrugged. "I'm not rich like most clean skins so I figure it's easier to just live where I work"

"So we're not going to your place?"

Kit attempted to look devastated. "No, but I can show you something way more exciting."

A distant roar traveled over them. Josephine craned her head past Kit and saw a huge mob of people circling and cheering around something that looked like a basketball court but without the hoops or the lofting basketballs.

"Where are you taking me?" She had forgotten about seeing his house. She figured he was still embarrassed and was willing to not make him go through with it for the time being.

Kit dragged her without answering knowing what he was about to show her would be way more interesting and insightful than him attempting to explain it. As they edged closer, the energy of the crowd grew palpable, and the sheer number and density became very real.

Kit pushed his way through the curtain of onlookers, never once letting go of Josephine's hand. It felt like they were passing through a porous wall as the crowd cheered and yelled until finally they reached the other side, revealing a basketball court divided into six parts width ways. Kids stood in each designated sixth of the court whilst one child stood at the end priming himself for what was obviously going to be a dash for the other side. People lined up at the edge of the court, six deep, screaming and exchanging bets.

Josephine was mesmerized—the intensity, the excitement, the raw emotion on display was so visceral and filled her with all sorts of untapped energy.

Kit leaned over. "It's called Border Cross, nobody knows who started it. They think the game came from someone who had family in Myanmar, but basically that kid must get to the other side without being tagged."

Josephine had one eye on Kit and one eye on the action. "And what do we do?"

Kit smiled back as if he was about to share some time-honored secret. "We bet."

Surrounded by rogue hands and exchanging money, Josephine couldn't get a word in edge ways, even with her public speaking prowess, between the desperate people gambling and the bookie trying to keep everyone in order. She was no match for the chaotic energy. She yelled back at Kit. "Who am I betting on?"

He yelled back. "The kid in the Lakers Shirt!"

Before Josephine could verbalize her bet, her money was snatched, and she was shoved a ticket before she was spat out by other people wanting a piece of the action. As the two of them lined the side of the court, the kids were lined up at the base whilst the others planted their feet ready to guard their blocks.

A random voice yelled out, "Go!" and like a collective wave, everyone jumped up as the kids raced for the other side. The intricacies of the game were laid out for Josephine as the indecisive kids were caught whilst the ones fully committed blazed through. The Lakers kid was a vision as he dodged and weaved with ease past the slow-moving grabs of the other kids. At the final block, it was just now him and another child left to do it all over again.

Josephine was getting caught in the excitement and Kit couldn't help but look over and be more in love with her than ever. The Lakers kid made another run for it, every step making Josephine squeal and cheer, "*Go, go, go!*"

As the Lakers kid reached the final block, he deployed a trick Kit had seen before as he pretended to be tired allowing one of the kids to overcommit.

Contorting his body, he avoided the tag and rushed for the end of the court to Josephine's cheers. "*Go, go, go, oh my God!*"

She turned to Kit who was beaming. He liked that she was enjoying herself.

"I won!" She hugged Kit and fanned herself as the Lakers Kid doubled over attempting to pull in a lung full of air. Moments later, Josephine thumbed through her winnings. "This is so weird. I've never felt currency before. How would we even spend this?"

"I got an idea, but before that. Hand that over for a sec," Kit said.

She handed over her winnings as Kit picked off a few notes. She watched him as he handed the kid the money along with everyone else who had won off his feats.

Coming back, Kit clapped his hands. "Let's eat."

The view of the city was unmatched from the top of the towers. Kit and Josephine sat on a weathered bench that had clearly been dragged from a kids' playground. Between them was a collection of fast food bags—burgers, onion rings, fries, and thick shakes. Josephine slowly chewed the food, savoring the out of this world flavors.

"What do you think?" Kit asked her.

"This food is all so salty." She laughed still amazed at the impact it was having inside her mouth.

"Yeah, we like to call it flavor. Here, try this." He grabbed a few fries and dipped them into a soft serve sundae before holding them up.

Josephine yanked her head back in astonishment and disgust. "No, that's where I draw the line, you can't combine those two foods."

Now Kit was perplexed. "Says who? Come on, trust me."

Josephine reached for them and tentatively put them in her mouth. Carefully, she chewed them as if she was tasting poisoned food for royalty. Slowly the combination of the salt from the fries and the sweetness of the ice cream created a bomb of flavour and texture that was both undeniably delicious and simultaneously addictive. "Okay, now that's making sense, unreal." There was something about Josephine taking in all these experiences that filled Kit with joy. He was coloring in a part of her that was blank; hopefully with colors that she hadn't used before. She was no doubt doing the same for him too.

"So how did you know about this?" she asked.

"The french fries?"

Josephine chuckled. "No, the rooftop."

Kit's face turned serious, or at least reverential and it didn't go unnoticed by her. "This is where a lot of Rats go to die, you know spend their last moments. It's the first place we look when the apartment is empty."

Josephine looked out to the city. "I've never seen it from this view before. Where do you live?"

Kit didn't respond immediately. He still had food in his mouth. "Where do I live?"

"That's what I asked." She wanted to make sure that she hadn't forgotten that they had not visited his house, that he had somewhat broken a promise.

Kit pointed. "You see that set of buildings over there…"

Josephine followed his finger. "The brown towers?"

Kit nodded. "Yeah, Those, I live in those."

Josephine wasn't expecting him to point out another set of towers. She'd be lying if she said she wasn't somewhat a little surprised—even a little concerned—was this guy actually too real for her? Or was she not real enough for him? Or maybe she was just scared of what she didn't know.

She had to give some kind of response so offered a neutral, "Uh huh."

Kit saw right through it immediately. "That's usually people's response."

Now she felt like an arrogant ass.

"No, I didn't mean it like that, it's just you live a very real life."

Kit smiled at the term real, "It's the life I was given." Her comment felt like a polite way of saying he was less than, but he had to keep reminding himself that he wasn't being truthful with her so he couldn't pull her up on stuff she hadn't been made aware of. "Is that why you're dating me? To feel more real?" He added a laugh at the end to make sure she knew he was joking.

Josephine caught the humor. "Yeah… you do, it's not a bad thing at all. Also you're really hot."

"So it's just my looks hey?"

Josephine smiled, glad that she had taken a little jab at him too. Also it was a good reminder that this guy could actually take a joke. Clean Skin guys were usually so self-serious. They were carefree but had, over the years, developed some bizarre aversion to self-deprecation. They were at once the securest guys around and the most insecure.

"Well, someone had to be the brains," responded Josephine which got Kit cackling.

"Hey, I got other talents," he responded.

"Yeah like what?"

"Ceramics."

She didn't know whether to believe him, the mere word made her burst out laughing. "Bullshit."

He nodded with a confidence that clearly indicated he was not mucking around. "Yeah, my Nan taught my parents, and they taught me, it was a hobby of mine."

Josephine stopped laughing and just sat in the visual of this well-built dude gently caressing a pottery wheel. It turned her on, the emotional balance of this guy, at once tough and carefree but also sensitive enough to want to craft things with his hands. "Is it still a hobby?"

Kit wavered. "Occasionally."

The two of them sat there silently for a moment, both surprised but glad at the direction the conversation had gone.

"So, could you make me something?"

It was the question Kit had been waiting to be asked. "Of course."

It was the answer Josephine had been waiting to hear. The fact that this guy was going to make something with his hands that would last forever had her thinking all kinds of thoughts—most of them were urging her to kiss him. She leaned over and did just that and Kit reciprocated. It was a long kiss further made special by where it was happening and the fact that she had gotten to know him more in an afternoon than she had over the past few months.

The sun was beginning to set. Kit and Josephine walked hand in hand through the Rat side of town.

Josephine's eyes darted from one spot fire to another—whether it was people fighting, loiterers, police, or the litany of cash for gold and gun shops. It was all too uncontrolled. The church in which she held her sessions with the kids was situated on the border of both sides of the city, so never in her life had she ever been this ensconced in Rat culture. She didn't feel unsafe because of the confidence in which Kit navigated these streets. But she did feel exposed, as if visiting a foreign city for the first time. Not that she knew that feeling firsthand but had heard stories from other travelers—that feeling that everyone is staring at you because they can tell you are a tourist.

As they walked, a car slowly idled next to them. Kit looked over as the window wound down, revealing Detective Flint.

"Hey there." Kit played it cool and figured it would be best to try and get the interaction over with as soon as possible. "Hey, I just gotta talk to this guy, I'll be back in a minute."

Josephine took a look at Detective Flint who seemed to be taking an invested interest in her. In his time, he could smell a Clean Skin from a mile away, and before Kit had even reached the window, he knew he had Kit right where he wanted him.

"Hey." Kit made sure Detective Flint was aware of his displeasure.

"Woah, what's with the tone? I just wanted to say thank you for ratting out that chick in the closet."

Kit didn't believe him for a second. "Sure, what do you want?"

The detective laughed. "You're right. Word has it you were at that party with your two dipshit friends."

Kit shook his head. "Negative. Was with my Nan."

He leaned out of his window to make sure Kit could see that Josephine was now the topic of conversation. "She looks a little too well bred for these parts. Maybe we should meet her. Do a random scan. What do you think?"

Kit felt powerless and realized his only way out of here was to play collaborator. "Or we can just… be cool, you know the going rate for cool?" He looked behind to make sure Josephine wasn't watching.

It was clear by the way they chatted that this was a typical exchange between jaded law enforcement and a powerless Rat. Kit pulled out a wad of cash and handed a bunch of notes over to the detective.

He cooly pocketed them. "That's all it takes, buddy." He changed his tune as if the whole exchange was fair and legal.

Kit suppressed every impulse he had to reach over and choke him with the automatic window.

"Well you two have a good day, you may want to bring her somewhere private before one of my colleagues decides they want to make a dent in their clearance rate." Detective Flint gave a little wave to Josephine.

This immediately made her feel uncomfortable—actually the whole exchange made her feel uncomfortable. Kit ambled back over to her. He offered a smile in a bid to diffuse what she just witnessed.

"What was that about?" Josephine asked.

"He's investigating a dead body we found at one of the houses. Come on, let's go before it gets dark."

Josephine sat on the edge of her dorm's bathtub. Kit sat inside, his shirt was off, his shoulder clean, still not showing any signs of his Nox Anima stamp.

Josephine's legs straddled either side of him as she tousled his hair. "About my father—"

Kit interrupted. "He was just doing his job," he said, waving it off.

Josephine picked up the head trimmer and clicked it on. It emitted that harsh buzzing sound. "So how do I do this?"

Kit turned slightly. "Does it have a number 1 on the clip?"

Josephine inspected it. "Yep."

Kit nodded. "Okay well just start rolling it over my head, pretend you're shaving your legs or your cha cha."

She hit him. "Hey!"

He chuckled.

Josephine started rolling the trimmer over his head, tufts of hair fell over his face along with that satisfying sound when segments of hair were cut. Kit rubbed Josephine's leg and smiled. Josephine found herself in a rhythm with the trimmer and enjoying the cathartic motion that came with pushing it backwards and forwards; the act was simple, non sexual, yet was easily the most intimate the two had been so far.

It was barely morning and Kit rocketed upright gasping for air. He looked around. It took him a moment to realize that he was still in Josephine's dorm. The sun filtered through the windows, and bathed them both in a morning glow that helped Kit regain his bearings and feel safe again. Josephine was still asleep. She was peaceful. It was one of those moments Kit knew would stay with him for a long time. Out the window, the noises of the campus grew. It was waking up.

Kit lay back down and faced Josephine. Eventually her eyes flitted and she began to wake up.

It made Kit smile. "Hey."

She looked at him and didn't say a word, she just smiled.

Kit wanted to know what she was thinking. "What?" He smiled.

She just smiled back. "You're very special to me."

Kit face grew red. "You're very special to me too."

Josephine closed her eyes, she was processing something ."So… ah… look, I want to tell you something and it's totally okay if you're not there yet…"

Kit was trying to muscle down a smile but he couldn't. He knew exactly what Josephine was trying to say and was so excited to hear it because he felt the same way. He figured if he was going to be truly vulnerable in this relationship, then he would have to say it first so he blurted it out. "I feel the same way."

Josephine let out the biggest of sighs, her hand on her chest, "Okay…"

Kit smiled. He relished in watching her bathe in the newfound discovery that he loved her, then he went one step further. "I love you, Jo."

Josephine giggled. "I love you, too, Kit."

The two of them said nothing more and just reveled in each other's words and soaked in each other's expressions. Josephine moved in and the two of them kissed deeply. She pulled back and took in his whole face. Now that it was out there, he looked different to her, like he had leveled up somehow and had become even more handsome, more unique. She just wanted to consume him and be one with his body. After kissing him again, she got up and went to the bathroom.

Kit sat up, processing what just happened. He closed his eyes for a few seconds and sat in that feeling he'd been searching for ever since Gem had succumbed to Nox Anima. Lifting his right arm, he rubbed the sleep from his eyes and noticed a blue flash. Leaping out of bed, he furiously checked his shoulder. There it was, his Nox Anima stamp blazing through his skin. The bathroom door began to open. Kit scoured the room for cover. By the time Josephine was looking up, she found Kit standing there, eyes wide, as if he'd just hit a deer. He was wearing a t-shirt with no pants—a look that totally went against the raw, roguish energy she was so attracted to, but she thought nothing of it.

"I gotta go to class, but are we still meeting tonight?"

Kit nodded nervously, but didn't say a word. Josephine went back into the bathroom initiating him to kick into gear and throw his pants on as quickly as he could as to not leave anything to chance. The whole scenario was a rushed panic and as that last leg went into his pants, something fell out of his pocket and hit the ground… the signal jammer. Its thunk on the carpet was too quiet for Kit to notice. Worse yet, it rolled halfway under the bed.

Grabbing the rest of his stuff, Kit called out to Josephine who was already in the middle of her shower. "I'll see you later… love you!" He took one last look around her dorm room before closing the door.

CHAPTER 18
EVERYTHING COOL?
NO IT'S NOT

Kit sat in his room. Unlike in Josephine's dorm, the sunlight streaming through just didn't have the same effect; that warmth was absent. Kit smashed down a red bull and a cylinder of Pringles. Every slurp and munch was frenzied. He typed away on a laptop, searched, scrolled then repeated. The words on the search bar read *Anima Balancer*. A definition popped up. Kit craned his neck forward and focused on the explanation.

An Anima Balancer is a term used to describe someone who performs an illegal procedure by which the patient has their Nox Anima stamping ring permanently removed, either by being cut out or reprogrammed.

Kit sat back. He knew he was running out of options. He had spent the last hour turning the house upside down looking for the jammer and had now conceded he had lost it yesterday amongst the chaos of the games. It didn't matter anyway, the jammer was becoming less effective by the day. He had two choices: tell her, or go through and find himself an Anima Balancer. Both seemed like no win scenarios, but the Anima Balancer at least meant he could keep what they had going. If he was to tell her the truth, there would be no reason for her to want to be with him, not because he had Nox Anima—she was too principled and good for that—but because he lied to her. He harkened back to when they first met and lamented why he just didn't show some guts. If she had walked away when he told her at the party then at least he would have known she wasn't right for him.

At that moment, Nan's voice called out from the bathroom. "Kit can you help me?"

Kit slammed the laptop lid shut.

He tucked Nan's shirt into her pants. She had just finished using the toilet. The look on her face was pure gratitude.

Kit pulled some pills he stole from Josephine's place out of his pocket. "I got something for you Nan."

Nan wasn't exactly enthused. "From who?"

Kit paused. "Ah a friend."

Nan chuckled. "So who is she, or he, or they?"

Kit tried to fain confusion, but he knew his Nan had a telepathic ability to read a situation. Maybe it wasn't so much telepathic as it was just her age and the wisdom that came with it.

He offered her a confused, "What?"

Nan gave him a smile, one that came when you

were playing chess with someone who was still playing checkers. "Kit, I'm losing my memory, not my mind. Unless your head shaved itself this time."

Kit conceded defeat. "Fair enough, I met this woman at a party."

"Is she like you?" Nan's question was quick; in fact there was no other question to ask in this world when two people met. Kit looked down

"No, she's not."

"Well, you better tell her then." Nan's response wasn't angry, or disappointed, it was just matter of fact.

"And if I do then what happens?"

Nan tried to reassure him with a hand on his shoulder. "It will either turn to shit, or it won't."

Kit kissed her on the forehead. "Get some rest," he said before he walked out of the bathroom.

At work, Kit and Jim were dismantling a bathroom that wouldn't have looked out of place in a night club. It had black round tiles that lined the walls and even the ceiling. The sink fixtures were gold and the basin was clear. It was all finished with a vanity mirror that was custom-shaped into the form of a diamond. Kit and Jim ripped out the fixtures with whatever tools they had. It felt sacrilegious to be ripping apart something that was so considered.

In the background, noises from the other removalists could be heard as they cleared and collected everything else of value in this dead Rat's apartment. A weird silence hung between the two best friends. Kit kept looking over to Jim but Jim never once looked back.

Kit cleared his throat. "So how's Tai?"

Jim kept his eyes on his task. "You bring my jammer back?" The question was followed by more silence. Jim attempted to keep working but eventually stopped himself and turned to face Kit. "*Kit, where is the jammer?*"

Kit struggled to face his friend. Quietly, he let out a response hoping he wouldn't hear it, "I lost it."

Jim laughed, but it instantly turned to rage. His friend had always been there, never let him down but if there was ever a time he needed him to stand up, it was now, and he hadn't. "You..." Jim wanted to call him every name under the sun but he refrained. His voice wasn't loud; it was just dense and weighted with disappointment and delivered in the most unflinching of manners.

Kit threw his hands up. "Man, I swear I'll..."

Jim sharked in. "You'll what? Find me another one? You know how impossible it was to get that one? You know why I got that jammer? I was gonna use it to sneak Tai and me into a Clean Skin restaurant. Get her one last proper meal. Like a dignified human. But instead she's gonna be sitting on the couch back at the apartment asking me why she's eating cold pizza!!" Jim screamed the last line, and it reverberated throughout the apartment causing every other removalist to stop what they were doing. The apartment went dead silent.

The Boss Man stuck his head in. "Everything cool?"

Jim took off his gloves and threw them to the ground, "No… it's not." He stormed out of the room, leaving Kit a hollowed-out mess.

The Boss Man looked at Kit. "Whatever that is, you damn well fix it."

Kit nodded silently.

Josephine held Kit's hand. He was leading her through the open doors of a noisy but homely feeling work-shop—the type of place that would host cooking classes with strangers.

Kit looked back at her, her eyes still closed. "Okay, open them."

She opened her eyes and instantly let out, "Ooh, no way."

Lining the walls were booths and tables with pot-tery wheels. It was a pottery workshop. "So what are we going to make?"

"Whatever that doesn't collapse on us," Kit responded as he tossed up a smile at the woman who was hosting the classes.

Josephine focused on the wet lump of clay as it rotated on the pottery wheel. Rust colored water slipped through her fingers as she attempted to contour the formless mold in her grasp into something practical.

Kit had his arms around her, his hands hovered over hers. "Okay that's it, just keep them steady. You ever seen the movie Ghost?"

Josephine didn't move her head, just her eyes towards Kit behind her. "No, is it about pottery?"

Kit smirked. "Not exactly. That's it just a light touch." He guided her hands upwards as the mold started resembling something that could be used as a bowl or a very wide cup. Kit was doing a good job of hiding the shame he felt from letting down Jim and appearing present, but really he was looking forward to the end of their date so he could go back to ruminating on Jim and finding a way to fix what he screwed up.

Kit looked down at his Clean Skin clothes—some of the clay had splattered onto them. He tried to hide his disappointment, not only did he need to hide his stamp but he needed to keep his Clean Skin wardrobe fully stocked now too. The forever accumulating elements required to keep up this façade was beginning to overwhelm him but he shook it off, knowing he only had to be present with Josephine for another forty-five minutes. He inspected what she had made. It looked like a bowl, only tilted to one side.

"Well it's certainly something," he said.

She could see Kit was ribbing her, but she liked it.

"How do I eat out of this thing?" He leaned his head to match the mangled angle of the bowl.

"Are you making fun of my bowl?"

"No, not at all, I think we all should be eating like this, on a forty-five degree angle, good for the digestion."

Josephine broke out into heavy laughter. Kit was proud he could make her laugh, that laugh made him forget about the rising panic that was starting to set into his chest.

Back home, Kit sat in his room. He had his shoe box between his legs and his back rested against his bed. He thumbed through the cash he had saved for Nan. He pulled out what looked like at least a quarter of the wad and counted it before crossing out the twenty thousand in the ledger and replacing it with a fifteen thousand. Looking at that money in his hand, he thought long and hard but ultimately, he had no choice. He was going to have to visit an Anima Balancer. There was that part of him that couldn't believe this was the length he would go to avoid telling Josephine the truth. He was kicking a can down the road and just figured if he could kick it far enough, that maybe he wouldn't see it for a while, and could just relax, enjoy the moments he had with Josephine, and when he reached that can again, he would figure something else out. Or maybe he would be dead.

Josephine sat with Elizabeth and their friends on the campus grounds. Their surroundings couldn't be more picturesque or at odds with what Kit was dealing with. Elizabeth was, as usual, holding court with one of her many stories. Josephine, on the other hand, was not present.

As Elizabeth continued, it didn't go unnoticed that her friend was somewhere else. She quickly finished her story and as the group continued with their conversation she leaned over and whispered, "Let's go for a walk"

Walking through the mass of students, Josephine took a giant breath. "I don't know what's going on… it seems like any time I want to get close to him, he has some sort of explanation to keep me at arms' length."

Elizabeth nodded. She wanted to interject, it was in her DNA to commandeer most conversations, but she knew better this time.

"I know he's not rich, in fact I think he's pretty poor, or even he's homeless, but I don't actually care."

Elizabeth knew her friend. "Don't you?"

"I don't… know. No, I wouldn't. It would be weird, but I like him, actually, I love him and he loves me… but… I don't know who I AM IN LOVE WITH if that makes sense."

The two of them kept walking—the only noise

between them was that from the hustle and bustle on campus.

Josephine nodded her head. "I shouldn't be talking to you about this, I should be asking one of his friends, but he doesn't have any, or doesn't want me to meet them—"

Elizabeth could see Josephine was starting to spiral. "Hey, look, I've never met this guy and I've seen you with every guy you've ever been with, and I've never seen you like this. Me I tell everyone, everything right away and that's just me, that's just the ADHD, that's how I operate."

It was the first time Josephine had seen her friend pull back the curtain on herself, and it made her feel special to be witnessing it.

"Now I guess that's just not him, doesn't mean he's a criminal or a bad guy, it just sounds like he has some stuff going on so I think the only way you're going to get there with a guy like that is if you ask him, point blank."

Josephine was utterly floored at the insight Elizabeth was displaying, as if it was a limited window of knowledge that would close the moment they stopped their walk. "Okay, that makes sense, and what if it is something bad?"

Elizabeth shrugged. "Then it turns to shit. But just remember you are entitled to feel safe and heard in this relationship, and there is only one way for that to happen."

Josephine nodded. "Thanks."

"You're welcome." Elizabeth reached in for a hug and the two embraced; it was a tender moment between the best friends, a leveling up of their friendship. That was before Elizabeth sneakily pressed Josephine's Our Cloud button and sprinted off laughing.

"Again." Josephine pleaded.

Kit stalked the aisles of a rundown electronics store. The windows were grimy and barricaded by criss-cross rusted copper bars. Shelves upon shelves offered up discarded tech equipment that most likely had been removed or stolen from deceased Rats. Cables, DVDs, computer accessories, modems, phones—it was really just all junk unless you knew how to build something out of it. He held a basket with an assortment of random items that he did not need, items that appeared to be placed in there with a different purpose.

When he walked to the front counter, an old man, someone whose first language wasn't English, rifled through Kit's basket. He placed each item carefully on the counter before taking an extended look at Kit. The old man reached underneath the counter and pressed something, which produced a light buzzing sound. The two of them stood there in silence but it was evident both

Kit and this old man knew exactly what was going on.

A succession of unlocking sounds came from behind a faux wall door that sat behind the counter. The door was heavily fortified, bizarrely so, it finally opened and revealed how thick it truly was—heavy enough for the person pushing it to struggle a little bit. That person was a thirteen-year-old girl. She was pasty, twitchy and wired, a kid of the cloud age. Instantly, she gave off introverted genius vibes but also someone who needed some serious vitamin D. She whipped her eyes up at Kit. "You got the money?"

Kit subtly produced his wad of cash.

The girl gave an approving nod. "Follow me."

The Old man lifted a false section in the counter. Kit stepped through and walked past the girl into the room as she nodded to him to keep walking.

Turning to the old man she barked at him in Russian, "Dad get food for after the procedure, I'm going to be hungry." She slammed the door, and locked it, producing that same succession of clanking sounds from the inside.

Kit looked around and it quickly became obvious that this kid was dancing to another frequency than most. The room lacked windows but felt human, thanks to the empty food containers and cans of energy drink everywhere. The shelves were covered in half constructed motherboards, laptops and smartphones. It wouldn't have surprised him if balancing Nox Anima was just a side hustle for this kid. On the wall were faded posters of brain diagrams and wrestling stars. A dentist chair sat in the middle of the room, which looked like it was stolen in a smash and grab job from the Clean side of town.

The kid dusted her hands off and, without looking at Kit, demanded the money. Her tone lacked any social grace. Kit offered her the wad and she counted it whilst looking up at him every few seconds.

"It's all there," Kit responded. Just seeing the money being counted made him wince. It was a financial blow to say the least. It wasn't a good idea—he knew it wasn't—but he just kept ignoring that voice in his head.

He looked over to a wall of screens that almost sent him into a fit of epilepsy. They were bright and loud and never stopped moving. One played a video game whilst another was relaying surveillance, and a third had on the wrestling. Moving his gaze over to the right of them, he spotted a Masters Degree in Engineering Science. Its frame was propping up something else; clearly this kid had no respect for higher education or the status quo.

"Sit down," she ordered.

Kit lowered himself into the dentist's chair. Leaning back, he spotted the kid's shoulder. It lacked a blue circle. This kid was entirely clean.

"People say you're the best." Kit's tone was weak, he

felt outmatched by this kid and was trying to do anything he could to break the weirdness her genius was creating.

"I know I am. You doing this for a job?"

Kit felt ashamed to say it but responded, "A girl."

The kid's face softened. "Is she hot?"

Kit nodded.

The kid nodded back with pride. This was why she did this. "Nice." She quickly shook it off and slid across the room in her wheelie chair collecting a blue phosphorescent drink in a plastic Mountain Dew bottle. She rattled it whilst wheeling herself back. "Drink this."

Kit reluctantly put the bottle to his mouth and started drinking; it surprisingly tasted okay.

"Don't worry, that drink is too important to taste like shit."

Kit caught a glimpse of something that looked like a jammer connected to a cellphone and thought he'd try for a second time to connect. "I've been using my own jammer."

The kid scoffed. "Those things are bush league. Your body gets used to the signal and adapts. Mine on the other hand runs on a random sequence that renews every two weeks."

Kit nodded pretending to understand.

"It's cool. You don't have to understand how it works, only that it does."

A sense of relief came over him, but moreso a sense of comfort. This kid was thirteen and could barely hold a conversation and yet somehow he was about to drop five grand on her to perform some of the riskiest surgery around.

"So this will get rid of the ring and cross permanently?"

The kid was still futzing with her equipment. "Only the ring, not the cross. Your cross is not a signal, it's an indicator, activated by the toxins released when Nox Anima is in its final stages." The kid chuckled.

Kit screwed his face. Apparently that was supposed to be a joke but all it did was make Kit feel apprehensive. "Ah maybe this isn't for me." Kit went to stand up but found his eyelids dragged him right back into the seat.

"Yeah, sorry buddy, you're not going anywhere. You drunk the drink, don't worry… it's going to be all right."

Kit moved in slow motion, his head tilted to the side where he faced an old Nox Anima propaganda poster from twenty five years ago. A young child stood there brandishing his bare shoulder. A giant smile on his face, the caption below him read: *Get yourself stamped today!* That was the last image Kit saw before he fell asleep.

Kit woke up in his own apartment scrambling at the sheets as he lifted himself upright. He assumed he was still in the weird kid genius' operating room but his familiar comforts and the natural light streaming in calmed his nervous system. Looking over at his shoulder, he noticed the bare skin where his stamp used to be. He tapped his shoulder, the stamp didn't react. He exhaled, and the relief of not having to deal with hiding that ring produced a smile on his face. Right now, in this moment, he was not going to think about the future.

Clean Skins' stores were more than a just stores. They were what you would call experiential. Everything was thought of—the music, the layout of the clothes, how you were greeted, the way in which things were folded and placed, the way the store smelled. Even the way you were guided and navigated around the clothes—big items first until finally you finished on accessories. The lighting was soft. You wanted to walk in feeling good and walk out feeling even better. This store in particular was called N.P.T. and it was where you would go if you were looking to go undercover as a Clean Skin. The clothes felt too on trend. If there was such a thing as fast fashion in their world, this was it.

Kit walked around. He knew if he could tick this box off, and grab a few outfits, it would go a long way to subduing that rising feeling of panic. Yet he didn't feel comfortable surrounded by this fashion. It felt like it

was judging him. It didn't help that most of the store
assistants looked at him and could sense he was slightly
askew. Looking up at the store mannequin, he decided
that it would just be easier to copy his style.

He approached a store assistant who wasn't rude but
wasn't warm. "Ah, could I just get what's on that mannequin, and that one over there too."

The store assistant sized him up. "Yeah, we may
struggle to have your size. You're not who we usually
sell to."

"Who do you usually sell to?"

The store assistant clammed up. To her, Kit was
clearly dressed like one of them—he was just built
denser. "Ah, I'll see what we have."

Kit stood at the register. The assistant rang up the
items, each one making a ding and each ding added to
that ever growing cost. Kit was eyeballing a sign which
read: *Cash not accepted. Any attempt to pay in cash will
result in law enforcement being alerted.*

Kit tensed up.

Finally the woman was done. "That comes to three
hundred and fifty dollars."

Kit nodded quietly. "Yeah, can I purchase this on my
Grandmother's OurCloud account?"

The store assistant thought nothing of it. "Yeah sure,
you have her access code?"

The color came back to Kit's face. "Yeah, it's Kristen

Dent, two one seven seven eight five four three four."

She processed the account. "And would you be okay if we made you're Nan an ambassador of this store? She can get discounts and stuff, or you can if you want."

Kit shrugged. "Yeah sure, why not."

Back at the Towers, Kit wheeled Nan around; it was their daily outing, a way for Nan to get some air. People nodded to both Kit and Nan, mainstays of these towers. "Hey Nan, I hope you don't mind but I used your OurCloud account to buy a few things."

Nan scoffed. "That thing still works?"

"Your pension goes in there."

"Whatever is left of it. So what did you buy?"

Kit didn't want to answer straight away. Nan looked back at him, he relented, "Clothes."

Nan got it immediately. "Still playing dress up for this girl?"

Kit pleaded. "Well, she sure as shit can't see me dressed like this."

THUNK!

Kit stumbled forward. Nan had ripped the breaks on him.

"Fuck Nan."

Nan sent him a look that he had rarely seen, and it made him feel not worthy of her company. "I'm not going to ask you again. Tell her who you are."

Kit tried to reason. "Nan…"

Nan was fired up. "Today." Her roar made it clear, this woman was a force back in the day. "Your parents didn't raise you like that… I'll meet you at the steps." She wheeled away leaving Kit to wallow in his shame.

A bunch of kids stood there, half smiling. They had watched the whole thing play out and wanted to rib this grown man who had just been chewed out by his grandma. Kit rolled his eyes and walked off. They looked familiar. As Kit passed them, it became clear who they were—they were the kids from Josephine's Youth Group. In particular Rex and Don.

CHAPTER 19
DO YOU LOVE HER?

Josephine and Kit both entered the hall of her youth group. The noise as always was that specific brand of chaos—kids eating, yelling, laughing and attempting to talk over each other, all of it without taking a breath whilst food fell out of their mouths.

Josephine looked over at Kit. "I like your outfit, N.P.T.?"

Kit was struck that she snuffed out his fashion sense. "You can tell?"

"Yeah, it's like what you would get if you searched Clean Skin look on your OurCloud, but you're pulling it off."

Kit twitched. He felt uneasy that she could see right through him like that.

Josephine called out, "People… let's take a seat."

The youths looked up and spotted Kit and went silent immediately. Rex and Don instantly recognized his face. They didn't know him, but they knew that face and looked at each other for confirmation. It was that adage, "You can smell your own type."

Josephine waited for them to settle in their seats. "Okay I want to introduce you kids to my partner Kitridge."

The kids continued to hoover down the junk food—most didn't give a shit—but Don clearly wanted answers, his unwavering, awkward, child-like eye contact said so. He shot a hand up. "So do you love her?"

Josephine quickly jumped in. "You don't have to answer that."

Kit was even quicker to jump in. "What do you think?"

The way in which he answered so quickly made Josephine feel protected.

Kit looked around. "You kids got any other questions?"

Rex threw a hand up. "Yeah, don't I know you from somewhere?"

Kit shrugged. "Don't think so man, I don't hang out with twelve-year-olds."

The other kids howled at the insult.

Rex was twelve but he was tough, he waited for the laughter to die down. "Yeah, I've seen you around the Flats."

Josephine butted in. "Kitridge lives there."

Rex wasn't satisfied. "Yeah, but you don't dress like that."

Kit didn't let the kid sweat him. "Don't know what to tell you, kid."

The earnestness from the kids was too hard for Josephine to ignore. She knew her kids well and could tell when something was bothering them. This was one of those moments.

Don stood up. "Prove it, show us your shoulder."

Kit looked over to Josephine as if to ask: *Is this kid for real?*

Josephine shrugged. Secretly she wanted him to show his shoulder but was also beginning to expect that he wouldn't as it would be more on brand with his semi-secretive nature.

Quickly she put an end to the accusations and quiet the voice in her head. "No, he's not going to…"

But before Josephine finished, Kit peeled off his top and showed the kids his shoulder. It produced a wave of silence that put the kids in their place.

Don shook his head. "No way! He's using a jammer!"

Josephine turned back to Kit, again that doubt began creeping in.

Kit could sense it too. "You think if I had a jammer, I'd be hanging around you kids?"

Luckily the kids agreed with his logic and started chiding Don.

"I'm going to let you kids in on a little secret. There is no such thing as a jammer. It's just a thing Clean Skins made up to give Rats false hope."

Don lowered his head. Kit had made his point.

Josephine had had enough. "Okay, we've seen his shoulder now. It's clean… let's move on. I don't think either of us would be stupid enough to break the law and risk going to jail."

Don shook his head. Nothing could rile a kid up more than when he knew he was right and told he was wrong, especially by an authority figure. He wasn't going to let it end like this. "You know I asked her out first." His statement carried all the toughness and defiance of someone who was sick of being pushed around.

Kit too had had enough and knew it was time to put a stop to this conversation. "And look where that got you."

That one retort sent the entire group into chaos, it was like Kit had pulled Don's pants down in front of everyone. Don waved him off and sat down and sulked as the other kids jostled him. Kit sent a smile to Josephine. She sent one back, just not as wide…

That night, Josephine couldn't get to sleep. The noises outside her dorm were loud. A party was happening somewhere but that wasn't it. What she witnessed today—that exchange Kit had with her youth group— had opened up a passage of thought in her mind that hadn't been open before, that passage was called doubt. But why now?

Everything about this guy made sense. He had the clothes, the name, most importantly he had no stamp. So what was she fretting about? Was it self-sabotage because she had finally met a dude who was basically perfect? Or was it because he hadn't filled in those gaps he promised he would—take her to his place, meet his people, basically introduce her into his world?

What he had done was pretty surface level and when Josephine dug deeper into those moments, there was no denying she actually didn't really know that much about him. She realized it wasn't going to happen unless she asked, like Elizabeth had advised. She sat up, figuring that she'd write the questions now so she wouldn't forget them in the morning.

Spinning out of bed, she dropped her feet and the sole of her right foot connected with the edge of something on her carpet. "Oww!" She pulled her foot up and there on the floor, with the moonlight glinting off its metallic base, was Kit's signal jammer. She needed a moment to make out what it was. She leaned over, picked it up and raised it to her eye level. Turning it on, it clicked into action. Lights, beeps and whirs followed. The contraption had her hypnotized and it took her a moment to put it all together—its shape, its size, the way it behaved… then it hit her.

Instantly, she felt light headed and gripped her bedsheets. Tears had begun to collect in her eyes and she wanted to burst out an unholy wail of pain but instead drew in a big stuttering breath which converted her anguish into anger. Pocketing the jammer, she threw on a pair of sweat pants and Ugg boots and stormed out of her dorm.

Josephine knocked furiously on the Elizabeth's door. The knock was impatient.

A few seconds passed before it opened, revealing a sleepy Elizabeth in her PJ's. "What are you doing here? I was trying to get an early night."

Josephine held up the jammer and immediately Elizabeth shook off what remained of her drowsiness. "What is that?"

Josephine dead eyed her best friend as if she should already know. "Take a guess… I found it under my bed."

Elizabeth's eyes widened, now she was awake. "No way."

Josephine paced around the room, the jammer in her hand; she kept looking at it, hoping it would offer more answers. Elizabeth was on her OurCloud scrolling through a directory.

"You're not going to find him, he hasn't got an Our-Cloud." Josephine's answer was delivered with impatience and disgust.

Elizabeth kept scrolling. "I'm not looking for Kitridge, I'm looking for Kit."

"Well, you're definitely not going to find him with a Rat name… wait a second, he was wearing clothes from N.P.T."

Elizabeth stopped scrolling. "So…?"

"They don't accept cash. He has to use a cloud to pay. Maybe he was dumb enough to become an ambassador. They're always hounding me to become one—"

Elizabeth was scrolling the N.P.T. ambassador list before the words had escaped her mouth. "Shussh!" She waved Josephine off to keep her quiet. She had reentered the zone.

Josephine looked down at the jammer again. Its sleek form represented not groundbreaking technology but betrayal.

"Found him, wait her..." Elizabeth's expression creased. "What was his last name again, Dent?"

"Yeah, it's Dent," Josephine spat out.

"Well there is only one Dent here. Kristen Dent, this woman is seventy years old, their newest ambassador, why is she buying clothes from this store?"

Josephine knew why and the answer had drained the life from her face. "Because she wasn't the one who bought them."

The revelation hit Elizabeth and she joined in her best friend's despair. She kept scrolling. "Well, she's either really dumb, or too old to care but her address is listed, Apartment seventy-five, Block Seven, Carlwood. That's the Flats."

Josephine stood there, her eyes red and glassy, she swallowed hard. "The Brown Towers."

Elizabeth stood up and gave her a hug. "I'm sorry."

In the clearing below the brown towers, the self-driving car gently eased its way to the center. Inside sat Josephine and Elizabeth, both peeking out the windows.

"People actually live here," Elizabeth said it as if it was the first time she realized the other half existed. It wasn't that she didn't, she just never needed to think about it.

Josephine looked at her. "Yeah, this is life for the other half, and it still deserves our respect."

Elizabeth shrugged. "See if you're still feeling that way when you confront him."

Josephine took a deep breath, one part courage one part nerves, two parts adrenaline. "Maybe park this up the street…" She stepped out and looked up.

The brown towers stood tall and defiant against the city landscape. They were old, decrepit and shit brown. A hollow wind rushed through which caused the most haunting of whistling noises. Without Kit by her side, she felt scared. These towers lacked the camaraderie of the other ones Kit had taken her too a while back. These felt hardcore, Clean Skins not welcome.

Stepping carefully, she attempted to locate tower block seven, but instead, found herself staring at a giant bedsheet draped across a bunch of windows with the statement *Baby please, catch my disease* written in savage red paint. Josephine lowered her eyes and began to move, one foot after the other, no break in the pace. As she made her way to Block Seven, the flavor of these towers made themselves apparent—a cry for help, a gang of youths mugging a helpless man; random gunshots as grown men sprinted away carrying goods; a domestic happening between a man and two women as they threw out his belongings from the window.

Spotting Block Seven, she scurried up the framework of steps, only lifting her eyes when needing to change direction. Some of the fly screens were open and she could see small kids sitting on the floor being blasted by daytime TV. Finally, she reached the balcony where she counted until she reached apartment Seventy Five. Quickly she rapped on the peeling wooden door. She took a quick look around. Luckily she was of no interest to anyone today.

The door partially creaked open. Josephine primed herself, ready to throw everything she had at Kit, then the door fully opened and, for a second, she couldn't see anyone, as if the door had miraculously opened itself. Then she looked down, and there sitting in her wheelchair was Nan.

"Hello."

Nan's open and calm demeanor floored Josephine to the point where Josephine struggled to spit out anything but a stammered, "Hi."

A pause sat between the two, Nan was happy to let

the youngster do all the talking.

Josephine composed herself. "Hi… I am Josephine, I'm—"

Nan interjected. "Dating my grandson?"

The response disarmed her. She stood there, imagining the conversations Kit had had with her, how did Kit describe her to his grandmother? For a brief moment, Josephine didn't think about the betrayal, or the deception, she just wondered what this woman thought of her, this OG pre Nox Anima lady. She looked back down at Nan and realized immediately that this woman wasn't the judgmental type.

"Come in, dear, I'll make you some tea."

"You'll have to excuse me if I start going off topic. I haven't taken my Alzheimer's pills, they make me sick."

But Josephine couldn't respond or move. The house, its furnishings, its design, its soul, all of it was too much for her to process in one glance. This is what the life of a Rat looked like; it was small, cramped, cheap and tacky regardless of how Nan tried to lighten the tone. The oppressive nature of these towers and their design were impossible to escape. Josephine struggled to focus on any one thing, photos, ceramics, trinkets. She zombied to a wall and followed a trail of photo frames that chronicled Kit as a happy go lucky kid with his parents until it reached a final one with Nan. He looked about eighteen and dressed like your typical Rat with the attitude to match.

Nan could see this information overload was affecting this poor woman. "Maybe you should sit down dear."

It took a long moment for Josephine to respond, she was literally learning about this guy, all over again, from the beginning, in real time and it was making her feel lightheaded. "Ah, could I use your bathroom?"

"Sure dear, it's down the hall."

Josephine didn't hesitate, she needed a reset. She splashed water on her face. It wasn't warm and didn't seem to be getting warmer, but it was what she needed to shock herself back into coherence. She let the droplets fall off her skin as she looked at herself in the mirror.

And like Kit asked himself over and over again when he was in front of the mirror, she asked herself, "What the fuck am I doing?"

After patting herself dry, she walked out of the bathroom and looked down the hall. Nan was wheeling around making tea. A gap of light sliced through the opening of a door. Under no accord of her own she headed for it. Her knees trembled at the thought of what she was going to discover inside. She wanted to cry but wanted the truth more. With her fingers, she gently pushed it open revealing Kit's bedroom.

Josephine's first reaction was her truest, shock. Everything in this room told a story, the story of a man she didn't know at all. Slowly, she started doing a perimeter check, beginning with the bowl of trinkets next to his bed. She scooped up a bunch of them, feeling the random assortment of textures before dropping them back in the bowl.

Leaning next to it was a photo of two people in what looked like a Mediterranean holiday spot, arms over each other. They were the same two people plastered all over the photos in the kitchen. Kit's parents. Josephine flipped the photo, on the back was some writing scrawled in pen, it read—

Hey Ma, we made it to Tropea. Tell Kit we love him, off on our road trip up the coast!

She put the photo down and continued her tour of this guy's life, whoever he was. She made her way to the wardrobe and, like all the doors in this house, opened them slowly. By now, she was aware whatever was behind them was just another sign, another item, another effect that was the opposite of everything she was told and believed. The doors swung open revealing Kit's clothes, an entire rack of Nox Anima fashion, and to the left, hanging alone, the few Clean Skin clothes Kit had been wearing on their dates. She grabbed a pair of his Nox Anima jeans that were purposefully ripped. She ran her fingers over the fraying edges, and for a second, she imagined him wearing those jeans, what it would look like. She smelt his t-shirt. It had a different odor to it; it was rough, it had slight B.O. but not in a bad way. It was a scent he had been masking.

She turned around and moved over to his desk. On it sat a collection of useless technology that either looked stolen or bought from a pawn shop. DJ turntables, a laptop, a TV screen, headphones, tablets. Josephine's eye was drawn to another photo; it took pride of place. It was taped against the window. She pulled it off and brought it closer.

The photo was of Kit and two other people. They all looked happy. Kit dripped head to toe in his Nox Anima fashion. For the first time, Josephine was seeing him for the person he actually was. She wondered if he was the same person with them as he was with her.

Did he just change his clothes or was his outlook on life different too?

She put it down, then noticed the most shocking photo of them all. Kit, with a girl. Both were giving off only the slightest of smiles as if they had heard bad news and were trying not to let it ruin the moment.

Who is this girl? Is she still in the picture? What are their conversations like compared to ours? Does he have better chemistry with her? Is she more real than me? The flooding of self-doubt made Josephine's hand tremble.

Dropping the picture, she backed away and, THUNK, tripped backwards over Kit's bed. Scrambling to her feet, she looked around and saw Nan at the door. Nan's expression was of pure sadness, as if to say *I'm sorry you found out this way.* Josephine stormed past her and slammed something into the palm of her hand. As the door slammed shut, Nan looked down to find Josephine had given her the jammer.

Elizabeth stared at Josephine lying down on the other seat in the car in a near catatonic state. Josephine's eyes were glued to the glass ceiling, the clouds moved by. Elizabeth remained silent. There was nothing she could say. What could she say? She had watched Josephine go on date after date with countless Clean Skin boys only to have found that the one man who could miraculously occupy both sides to be a fake.

Maybe that's the problem, Elizabeth thought but was wise enough not to say out loud. There was just no such thing. You were either a Clean Skin or a Rat and if you tried to be both you were ultimately insulting the other side whilst simultaneously betraying your own people.

The car eventually stopped inside the campus. Elizabeth waited for a response, but Josephine remained with her eyes fixed on the ceiling.

"Um… you want to stay with me tonight?"

The response from Josephine was long and drawn out until eventually she mustered up a very slow, almost imperceptible shake of her head.

Elizabeth stepped out. "Please don't do anything rash."

The door clunked. Josephine looked to the wheel where a driver would usually be seated.

"Take me on a drive… anywhere."

On the outside, Elizabeth watched the self driving car zoom away and exit the campus. She stood there wondering where the car was going. She called out, "Josephine!" but her voice got lost in the wind that had picked up.

CHAPTER 20
SO THIS IS HIM...

Nan sat in her chair looking out the window. She wasn't in any mood to work the pottery wheel. She couldn't shake the utter disappointment in her grandson for not telling Josephine the truth. Maybe as someone who never had Nox Anima and grew up in an era that wasn't afflicted by it robbed her of that empathy to see both sides. But then again, lying was lying.

The door clicked open moments later and Kit called out, "Hey Nan, I'm home."

Nan didn't respond.

Kit walked into the kitchen. His eyes went immediately to the small dining table. Sitting there was the jammer. Kit halted in his tracks, his mind processing all the different variables of how this thing could have found its way back into his house. He did his best not to panic. Walking in to find Nan, her blank stare out the window, didn't fill him with much confidence. "Hey Nan, where did you find this?"

Slowly she turned to him, her expression didn't change, just blankness mixed with despondence. "Your girlfriend returned it. She was here." Nan wheeled off to leave him there to sit with his screw up.

Kit looked down at the jammer and gripped it tight before screaming out - "FUCCCCKKK!!!!" His roar bellowed out and ricocheted all over the tiny apartment.

Kit furiously rapped on Jim's apartment door. Slowly the door opened revealing Tai, supporting herself with a walking stick, wrapped in a blanket and that rash was now up her arm and neck. Nox Anima was casually taking its next victim. For a second, Kit had to recalibrate. He hadn't seen Tai in a long time and seeing her like this triggered memories of Gem and her last months fighting the mutation. Tai looked back and called out for Jim. Even the act of yelling was too much for her as it initiated a coughing fit. Kit stood in and she used him to prop herself up.

Breathing in, she produced a smile. "So, how's your lady?"

"Gone, she found out."

Tai raised an eyebrow. "You going to chase her?"

Kit nodded. "Yeah, I'm gonna try."

Jim appeared and Kit held up the jammer. Jim walked past him and closed the door on Tai.

The two of them stood in each other's silence for a moment. Kit handed him the jammer. It didn't bring the response he was expecting or wanting.

Jim looked at it and sighed deeply. "Great, too late, so what do you want?"

Again Kit assumed the return of the jammer would bring about a reconciliation but instead he was left flat footed and searched for his next words. "Um, actually, I gotta borrow the truck."

"No."

"What do you mean no?"

"Not for this, not for her." Jim's tone was bordering on disgust.

Kit had begun to break down, his eyes, his voice, his dropped shoulders. "You don't understand, I need this woman in my life."

"You already have a woman in your life". Jim shouted back with such fury that it made Kit take a step back. Jim was pointing back to Kit's apartment, obviously referring to his Nan.

For a brief beat, the two best friends realized that this was probably the end for them—both were broken over it, but neither could see a way to walk any of it back.

Jim sucked in any impulse he had that made his eyes want to water and weighed his words carefully. "If you are going to be with her, then I don't want to be with you." He turned around and went back into his apartment.

Kit looked down, he couldn't shake the shame. In that moment, it felt like he had lost everyone. Jim, Josephine and even the respect of his Nan.

A fist knocked on Josephine's dorm room. It was a hasty knock. The door opened revealing Elizabeth. Her face dropped immediately when she saw Kit. He stood there in his Nox Anima attire.

Elizabeth looked him up and down with the same contempt Jim had projected onto him only hours before. "So, this is him."

Elizabeth's tone made Kit feel small—no doubt it was her intention. But also seeing him for the first time humanized him. She didn't know who to expect, what he would look like, but he certainly was different to what she had pictured in her mind. She could see why Josephine was attracted to him. He was all X factor in a world of Clean Skins, but a little too gritty, a little too real for Elizabeth's tastes.

Kit brushed past her and started searching the dorm. "Jo, Jo, I just want to talk."

Kit paused after a few seconds. Something wasn't right, something felt different—the couch, the posters, the layout. Was this even Josephine's dorm?

"We swapped dorms. She's in mine now, so you'll never find her... again." Elizabeth couldn't be more pleased with this reveal.

Kit couldn't give a crap. "Who are you again?"

Elizabeth's face dropped. She took a few steps forward, puffed her chest out, ready to teach this lying Rat a lesson. "I'm the friend who doesn't break Josephine's heart. You must be the other one."

She had nailed him in one sentence. That look of loathing that was following Kit around returned.

"Why aren't you people ever happy with what you've got," she snarled. It was one of those quintessential statements from a clueless Clean Skin that basically was code for, *Go away and die, you're lucky we let you have this much in life.*

Kit was ready to launch a full-scale defensive on her but knew better of it. Nothing was going to be achieved here. Forging past her, he bumped her on the way out.

"Classy" Elizabeth yelled out.

In the middle of Campus, Kit stood dead to the humming waves of cool and calm students strolling past him. His Nox Anima attire made him stand out to the point it looked like he was there to perform a one man play and he had just changed into costume. Some of the students took notice, others didn't, but it didn't matter because Kit was numb.

A gentle hand gripped his shoulder. "Sir, I'm going to have to ask for your student pass."

Kit didn't respond immediately. He just nodded, knowing that this humiliating exchange was, in effect, the perfect end to all of this. "Yeah... maybe you should just show me the exit."

The security guard wasn't there to make a scene. He just nodded Kit over in a direction. "I'll take you there."

On multiple occasions, Kit tried to call Josephine. His calls were met with a pre-recorded alert telling him his number had been blocked. Josephine, on the other hand, struggled to stay attentive and engaged with her Youth Group. A conversation would quickly spiral into a bickering match between the kids and leave Josephine emotionally taxed and unwilling to stop it.

Over the next few weeks as time passed, neither Josephine nor Kit were present in anything they did. One of them wanted answers and an apology—the other wanted to explain and apologize. But neither were truly ready to begin the process. Neither had felt this way about someone in a long time and didn't know if they could get that feeling back, whether it be with each other or the next person they date, so the safest thing to do was just not bother with the feeling ever again.

Whilst the standoff between the two lovers continued, Jim was preparing the festivities for Tai's Death Day party—a rite of passage for anyone with Nox Anima, a time where the Death Dayer would get hopped up on as many drugs as possible in a bid to fight off the mutation's final effects so that person could dance, booze and celebrate one last time. A roller door opened revealing an empty warehouse. Jim looked around and nodded his head. He was going to make this goodbye as epic as possible after losing the chance to take her out with the jammer.

Kit was washing Nan's clothes, despondence had become his entire physicality now. The way he scrubbed the clothes, his posture, the lack of emotion on his face—gone was that sturdiness, that confidence. It was as if his Nox Anima had activated without activating. In short, he was defeated.

"Kit, are you in there?" Nan called out.

"Yeah," Kit responded back blankly.

Nan wheeled herself in. "What are you doing?"

Kit didn't look back. "Killing time."

Nan probed and wheeled around trying to make some eye contact. "Have you apologized?"

Kit didn't want to have this conversation, but Nan was blocking the door. "She won't let me."

Nan shook her head. "Well, you're not trying hard enough. How do you expect to get back together?"

Kit spun around. "We're not getting back together. You understand? It's not happening, and if it did, and I got arrested, what would happen to you?"

Nan let him have his tantrum. She always knew how to diffuse a situation by not reacting. "I guess someone else will have to start saving for my future."

Kit was stunned. "What???"

Nan's smile was warm and reassuring, when it could have been smug, but she was too good for that. "You think I didn't know? I'm here twenty-two hours a day. I know everything. Even if I forget it sometimes. I'm not going in a home."

Kit finished up with the washing. "I made a promise to Mum and Dad."

"Well they're dead Kit"

The bluntness of her response made Kit want to cry.

"Have been for a while now, so make a promise to me instead. Apologize to that girl. And never save another dollar again. You got that?"

The trestle tables were piled with food, a lot more than usual, and it wasn't only the amount but the type—chips, candy, soft drinks, hot dogs, cake, cupcakes and not a vegetable or dip in sight. In the middle sat a three-tier birthday cake that read *Happy 13th Birthday Tan* and next to it sat a gaudy gold watch in a box. The watch was clearly a fake but it didn't matter to these kids. The watch was the first step in a tween's journey to becoming an adult with Nox Anima. It signified the moment where your time was taken a little more seriously, not only by those around you but by yourself.

Some kids stuffed their faces with food whilst others danced to the music. It wasn't just the Youth Group that was present but nearly half the neighborhood kids and even some of their young parents. One of them grabbed Josephine by the arm and dragged her inside the dance circle. Josephine started moving with the beat to the encouragement of the kids.

As if sensing his chance, Don entered, mustering every bit of smoothness he had learned over his twelve years. He started dancing with Josephine which elicited a thick wave of hooting from the kids. For the first time, Josephine was back in the moment and comically Don thought he had a chance, but as quickly as that moment came, it was lost when Josephine spotted someone at the door.

The kids, noticing the change in her demeanor, all turned with her to face a sheepish-looking Kit, dressed as a typical Rat.

Don stepped forward in all his tween bravado. "See, I told you. Want me to kick his ass?"

Josephine put a hand on his shoulder. "It's fine, Don… but thank you." She made her way over to Kit.

Don remained in a dead eye stare before Tan pulled him back into the dance circle.

In a dimly lit hallway just outside the main room, Josephine and Kit stood there and listened to the muffled music and chattering kids. There was no way this conversation was going to end well so neither were game to start it. But if this was where this conversation had to happen—in this dank, dark hallway—well this was where it had to happen.

Josephine inspected his clothes. "So this is you?"

Kit nodded his head. "Yeah, this is me, but I was also me when I was with you."

Josephine breathed in deep and closed her eyes. "And that girl in the photo?"

"Gem." Kit said her name with a level of reverence she wasn't expecting.

"She your girlfriend?"

Kit took a moment. "Was. She's dead."

Josephine wasn't expecting that answer but a sense of relief washed over her knowing at least he hadn't been cheating. She felt she at least needed to offer some condolences. "I'm sorry, I assume she was pretty special."

Kit nodded, tears welling in his eyes. "She was, but ah… let's just say meeting you helped me move on from her, a lot more than I could have imagined…"

Josephine struggled to stay mad at him, but knew she had to keep him accountable for any sense of closure. "I want to see it."

It took Kit a second to understand what she was getting at; he slowly peeled up his sleeve to reveal his clean shoulder.

Josephine searched. "Where is it?"

Kit exhaled. "It's gone."

"So where is it?" Her voice was demanding, she

wanted to see it on him—if this was the real him then it should be all of him.

"I got rid of it."

"You used a signal jammer to hide it from me?"

Kit nodded. "I did, then it stopped working, so I paid for a procedure to have it removed from my shoulder permanently."

Josephine stood there hollowed out, like a breeze could blow through one ear and out the other. She replayed all those moments when Kit's shoulder was on display. Even though there was no way she could have known, she felt fooled. None of it felt like it was done in the name of love. "You know my friends told me I should press charges, slap you with a fine and a restraining order, even send you to jail." She said it as if she had made a mistake not doing it.

"Yeah, I appreciate that." Kit was struggling to make eye contact. This wasn't a discussion. Kit was getting a dressing down, one that he deserved but wasn't conditioned for.

"You know Kit, that's your actual name right?"

Kit nodded, his eyes were still glassy.

"Well this is the type of thing you tell someone, preferably on the first date."

Kit scoffed. "Easy for you to say, this is not your problem."

Josephine shot back. "Of course it's my problem!!"

Kit arched his back and faced Josephine, a resolve had come over him. "Yeah for how long? A few months? And then when it all gets too real, what happens? It's simple, Josephine. I'm gonna die, you're gonna live, and if they catch us, I'm going to jail, not you, I was protecting you"

"No you were lying to me"

The two of them stepped forward knowing there was no going back now.

"Out here, it's the same thing. This isn't a game. You don't get to come into our world and pat some Rat kids on the head and host a few protests and then leave when it gets hard."

Josephine barked back. "Hey fuck you. You listen here, you asshole. I did nothing but love you for who you were, and you did nothing but lie to me about who you were not!"

Kit knew it was her turn now.

She continued, "I'm not trying to pretend that your life hasn't been all kinds of shit, but I'm sorry, that isn't my fault. And I won't let you blame me for that. I won't! If you had actually let yourself feel the pain you are supposed to feel, we wouldn't be in this mess. You would have let me feel it, too. That's how boyfriends and girlfriends work"

Kit waved her off. "You don't get to feel the pain. That's the beauty of your life. So stop feeling guilty as if Nox Anima is your fight. Dating me isn't going to fix that. It's not my job to give you credibility. You're still you. So have the guts to own that shit, walk away and live the next eighty five years because seeing you around these parts is a fucking insult to all of us."

Boom. She slapped him. Kit's eyes rolled upwards, a high-pitched sound whistled in his ears similar to tinnitus as he staggered backwards holding his cheek. For a second, it worked, the voltage in the exchange had been discharged as the two of them stood there drenched in the anger of the last few minutes.

The words cut Josephine deep because she knew there was an ounce of truth to them, but equally, Kit knew what he just said was spectacularly unfair. It was too late now. He had said them—a by-product of someone who was always fighting to be heard.

Josephine couldn't look at him. She let his words sit there and hang. He wished he could take them back, but she was too mad now to let him.

"…I can't believe you said that." Her words came out softly, her tone was someone who was exhausted by the exchange and frankly surprised at how this conversation had played out.

Kit knew he had fucked up, not only by lying to her but failing to apologize. She walked away and left him there. The clunk of the door brought in the sound from the birthday crowd, but just as quickly sucked it out and with that this defining chapter of Kit's life. He stood there ready to cry but sucked in the tears like a true Rat, and instead, began to punch the brick wall behind him.

CHAPTER 21
FIND THE GEMS

The warehouse that Jim had unlocked earlier was now decked out completely for Tai's Death Day celebration. Whatever decoration—whether it be balloons, crepe paper, streamers, cups—was all in the theme of black and silver. Kegs of beer lined the walls, bottles of spirits lined the tables. Not a scrap of food in sight, it was not going to be that type of party. Kit and Jim had been to a bunch of these.

Kit rolled in another keg. Then he stopped and looked around. He remembered Gem never wanted one of these parties. She wasn't that type of person. She was happy to retreat into the background. That was what made her passing that much sadder. Kit was the only one who really got to hold the memory of who she was. He wished she had let more people in but her introverted nature was also what made her, her, and the woman he fell in love with.

Jim watched Kit, who was lost in his thoughts. It was hard to tell if these two had made up and if Jim had forgiven him. Kit was struggling to stand the keg upright.

Jim had seen enough as he rolled his eyes. He strode over and helped his former best friend lurch the steel drum to a standing position. The two dusted off their hands and hung around in each other's awkward presence.

"It's always going to be messy between us and them. Sometimes words just aren't enough to make it work." Jim put a hand on his shoulder and gave it a soft shake.

That phrase, "Sometimes words aren't enough" halted Kit. It had him racing in thought, sparking something inside him, an idea, but he couldn't move until he had processed what it meant and what he had to do.

A lump of clay slammed repeatedly onto a bench, hard enough that the bench rattled underneath it. It slammed again and again, with force, as if rocketing in from the cosmos above. Each time it hit, the clay lost just a little more of its integrity until finally Kit's hands dived in and started kneading it to the right temperature and density. His right hand reached over and flicked the switch on the wheel that was caked in dry clay. That familiar sound rang through the apartment, that metronomic whirring that could lull you to sleep.

Kit tossed his mound of clay onto the wheel and cupped his hands. It was the first time in a very long time he'd made anything for anyone. The familiar feeling of the clay between his fingers and the mindfulness required to shape what he had pictured in his mind gave him comfort.

Nan wheeled in. "What are you making?"

Kit remained focused on his clay and the wheel. "An apology."

Josephine sat in a lecture theatre. It was a panel discussion between her and another three students. Behind them was the topic of the discussion projected on the board: *The fight for societal reunification.*

The theatre was three quarters full with students taking up the first twenty rows. Josephine felt somewhat more present than she had been the past month. That fight with Kit in the hallway—although not bringing the outcome she wanted—did let them both voice their grievances with the situation. Basically, it alleviated a certain level of heaviness that she had been carrying. Also, for the first time in a long time, her appetite had returned. The turmoil of their break up had made her feel sick in her stomach, and everything she ate was solely for the purpose of sustaining herself. The joy of eating had gone because love and thus the amplifier of the volume life had been taken away but now she was clawing her way back to becoming whole again.

Suddenly a question was thrown her way by the moderator. "Jo, you said at a rally last month that *Nox Anima is not just a lack of time, it is not having the capability to realize one's full potential as a human being.* Do you want to expand on that?"

Josephine nodded. "Yeah… Um…" She couldn't find her words, the question had triggered something inside of her, a pattern of thinking that was unexplored. "Yeah, what I would add to that is that potential is not just a singular thing. Potential can be realized in our exchanges and collaboration with people, especially those with Nox Anima, that is if we get the opportunity to get close enough to them, and yeah it's probably going to be uncomfortable and messy but what's the alternative? We already know what this life of ours as Clean Skins has to offer. We're not learning anything new, that only comes from challenging ourselves." She had forgotten the question, or even that she was part of a panel discussion.

The panelists, the moderator, the students all looked at her as if she had had a stroke. Josephine sat there wondering if she had just convinced herself to forgive Kit.

The sun dipped down and rose again like it did any other day. Kit sat up on his bed. He had the tired eyes of someone who clearly spent the night ruminating. Turning to his window, he watched different flats and residents start their day. He wondered, why did his day deserve to have a happy ending, to have Josephine part of it?

Maybe it doesn't, he thought, *maybe I should just give up and let the rest of my days play out like everyone else, I'm no different.*

Nan passed his room and, without stopping, said to him, "Get dressed and go say goodbye to your friend."

Josephine sat on her bed studying. She was better rested than Kit.

A pleasant chime pinged in her head, followed by a message. "Message from the student hub. An item is waiting to be collected."

She had no idea what they were talking about. She tried to recall any orders she made online but nothing came to mind. Slowly, she got herself off her bed, chucked on her Ugg boots, and made her way to the hub.

She leaned on the reception desk. The hub was as its name suggested; the place where students hung out. It was quiet today, most kids were locked away studying for exams. A young student searched through an array of pigeon holes before pulling out a brown paper bag.

"This was left for you." He handed it over.

Josephine felt the weight of it and the shape of it creasing the brown paper. "By who?"

The student shrugged.

"Thanks."

Josephine walked over to one of the couches and set herself down. She looked around again, wondering if the person who had delivered this item was also watching her to gauge her reaction. Slowly and carefully, she unwrapped it. As she pulled down the last covering of the bag, she revealed a ceramic bowl. It was perfect in its imperfection but executed by someone who had a gift for the art form. Inside the bowl was a card. She pulled it out and unfolded it.

Inside, scratched in pen were the words, *How do you tell the girl who makes you forget you are dying that you are dying? You just tell her and hope she can forgive you. Even if I couldn't have offered you forever, I could have offered you honesty. Have a good life, I know you're going to get it right. I am eternally sorry. Kit.*

Josephine closed her eyes and started crying.

Kit's fist banged on the warehouse door. The throb of bass from behind it was so thick that it was causing it to rattle off its fixtures. The door wildly swung open, blanketing Kit in a wash of hip-hop music and a huge partying crowd. Kit stalked in. He was wearing his best Nox Anima gear, and so was everyone else at the party. By the sheer numbers and the lack of personal space, you could have sworn the entire population of the Flats were at this party.

A Death Day party was one of those occasions that brought the entire community together. Rats from every clique danced, drank and took as many drugs as humanly possible whilst putting aside any difference they may have had with each other. It was a testament to the person Tai was and the standing she and Jim had in the community. Kit navigated the crowd. Technically at his age, still without a Red Cross, he was considered the peak of Rat life—old enough to have some wisdom yet still young enough not to be dying.

Most people stopped and shook his hand and said hello. Yet amongst these folks, he made sure to hide his now missing stamp as he would have stolen the spotlight. As he passed every primal urge on display from people overtly making out to what surely was sex in the guise of dancing, he looked up and was hit by condensation dripping from the roof. That was how overfilled the warehouse was.

In the middle of the cyclonic celebration was Tai. She was the engine room of the party, drinking alcohol from a baby bottle slung around her neck. It was clear by her faulty steps that she had been propped up with as many pain killing drugs as possible, anything to let her enjoy this moment. She threw her arms out as Kit smiled. For a second, he totally forgot about Josephine and remembered that he actually had family who were in this mess with him until the end.

Kit wrapped his arms around her and gave her the biggest of hugs.

Tai pulled him back and took a good look at him, like

a proud parent. Her eyes were half closed as she battled hard to focus but wanted to make sure this came out right. "Good on you for trying. We deserve to love who we love."

Kit wanted to cry, but it was her party. He offered her the biggest smile behind glassy eyes. "You lived it better than all of us."

The two hugged again. From a distance, Jim watched, a warm feeling came over him. For this brief moment, they were a trio again.

Predictably though, as the party wore on, Kit felt more and more removed from the people around him. He started to think that maybe his brush with a Clean Skin had skewed his perspective, made him take stock of his life in a different way. He tried to get in, move his head to the music, get in on conversations but none of it felt right. These were his people but he was now a different person.

Suddenly, the lights turned on. White, unflattering fluro tubes flooded the warehouse. Everyone shielded their eyes.

The music had stopped and Jim was now on the stage looking around. "Where's Tai? Tai where are you!"

Murmuring followed as the crowds parted, and a bunch of friends led Tai to the stage. Her Nox Anima cross now a deep red, so deep it caught your eye before the blue ring around it, whilst the rash now covered most of her arm.

Jim helped her up and gave her a kiss. It was long and evoked the most monumental of cheers from the crowd.

Gently, he sat her down on a chair and whispered to her, "I'm so proud of you." He tried to feed her some more pain killers but she waved him off.

She didn't want them anymore, she wanted to feel the pain, feel it all one last time.

Jim handed her the microphone and even the weight of that seemed to be too much for her at that moment. Looking around, she absorbed the faces of all these people who had come to say goodbye. Everyone realized what she was doing because it was a tradition to do so—take stock one last time, look around, remember the faces, remember the times, bring as much as you could with you to the afterlife.

Then from the crowd a voice boomed out. "Stop wasting your time!"

The crowd laughed and jeered, a joke that never got old and was somewhat expected before the speeches.

Tai smiled and waited for the crowd to settle down again, eventually she was ready to say her piece. "There was a time tonight where for a couple of seconds I didn't feel the bad stuff. Didn't feel the rash, didn't feel the pain, the drugs, didn't feel the shit that I know is just around the corner."

Nobody dared to move including Kit.

Tai pointed to the middle of the warehouse. "It was over there, in the middle of all of you."

A cheer arose from the congregation.

"I don't have much to show for my life. I don't have any money… I don't have any real family, but I do have that moment. And I'm going to bring it with me into the darkness because it's the only good shit I have left."

The words had the group fall silent again as Tai wrangled with the heady combination of the painkillers, Nox Anima, and her emotions. She turned to Jim. He was silently crying and didn't care who saw it.

"You are more than the man who saved me. You are my partner. You helped me build this. From a piss weak little girl." Tai motioned to herself. "I'm not afraid of shit!"

The crowd cheered as Tai fought back what appeared to be her last ever coughing fit. "This is how I'm going to go! Right here, right now!" Another cheer rose as Tai stood up. "Celebrate the Gems!"

The crowd went nuts.

"Now play my song!"

And with that final battle cry, Tai collapsed, taking the chair with her. Kit rushed the stage joining Jim in propping her up. Tai was now borderline unconscious, barely alive as Jim slung her over his shoulder. Kit waved people away, urging them to form "The Guard." The crowd having done this before parted ways to make a corridor. Kit got himself under Tai's other arm and slung her over his other shoulder. Tears streamed down their faces onto Tai's as the two best friends carried their now dead best friend down the guard of honor. People reached out, putting hands on her arm, or leg, in a bid to say a final goodbye and touch her before the afterlife. The whole procession resembled the carrying of a Madonna statue down the main street of a crumbling, European town.

Tai's music played over the speakers. This tradition was one of those inevitabilities that no matter how many times you experienced it as a Rat, you were never prepared for it when it hit. Reaching the old, caged elevator, it was now Kit's turn to say goodbye. He pressed the button and the metal doors shanked open. Putting a hand on Tai's cheek, he said his final goodbye. Looking up, he locked eyes with Jim. Both knew it—with Gem and Tai now gone, it was only the two of them.

Jim carried Tai into the elevator. The doors closed, bringing a visceral finality As it rose upward, Jim bowed his head. Behind Kit, the guard of honor remained. The final bars of Tai's song played out to a solemn crowd before eventually giving way to a respectful silence that lasted for over a minute before Kit slowly turned to face the people. He took the deepest of breaths and looked over to the DJ and gave him the slightest of nods.

The DJ leaned into his mic. "To celebrate our fallen

sister, and her grieving mister, we're gonna play a tune that I think we can all agree means a little something to all of us." He kicked his turntables into gear launching into a heavy bass as if a switch had been flicked, electrifying everyone, who began dancing again. It was the only way to move on, to forget that this, without fail, would be everyone's fate eventually.

Kit looked around. He couldn't partake, it just wasn't in him anymore.

On the roof of the towers, Jim dragged Tai over to a bench. After sitting her down, he lay her head in his lap. It was sunset, the sun dipping behind the cityscape painting them in a brilliant purple and orange. Stroking her hair, he looked over the city he called home. Tai's left eye opened ever so slightly, and with her last ounce of strength, she soaked in the view before closing it and passing away for good. Jim looked down, sensing the life escaping her body. He let out a cry which quickly descended into a full fledged wail. It was the first time Jim had ever cried out loud in his life, and it would be the last. He had been saving it for her.

Back at the party, Kit was ready to turn around and take the elevator down himself. He was done. Nothing was to be gained staying and hanging with these people. While scanning the crowd one last time something hit him. These people were strangers. Sure, they all had one thing in common but the older he became, the smaller his world got, and now, it was as small as it could get, just him, Jim and Nan.

He reached over for the button on the elevator but something clipped the corner of his vision. He turned around and scanned the crowd again trying to find it, searching randomly, it hit him again and this time he locked on for dear life because he was not going to let it go. There in the middle of the crowd, looking directly back at him, was Josephine.

For a moment neither of them moved, they just watched each other, reveling in the fact that they were the only ones not moving amongst the hundreds of writhing party goers. She was dressed in a not quite Nox Anima style t-shirt and pants, her best effort to fit in but it didn't matter. By this stage everyone was too stupidly high to notice a poser. Gradually, the two of them pushed forward towards each other. Dodging, weaving and bumping through the crowds, they couldn't reach each other fast enough. As they got closer, their smiles got brighter, tears welled in their eyes until finally the two collided so hard and so fast they nearly headbutted each other.

Neither wanted to instigate the kiss. Instead, they leaned back to soak in the other person's entire face in totality. It had only been six weeks but felt like an eternity. Kit slowly leaned in and Josephine did the same until their lips met. What took place, could only be described as an atom bomb of emotion. It was the greatest kiss ever, and it created a protective dome, shielding them from all the harsh realities their love was destined to face. As the two stood there, making out amongst the chaotic post celebrations of Tai's life, it was evident that this was one of those "Gems" Tai was talking about.

CHAPTER 22
IT'S NOT MY CALL

It was the peak of night. The furthest possible time before the return of the sunlight. Josephine remained in a lucid state in Kit's bed. Stretching out an arm, she reached for him but found nothing. His absence shook her out of her sleep. Gingerly she looked around and sat up. There she spotted him across the room, sitting down, staring into a mirror, underneath the shine of a lamp. She climbed out of bed, she walked over. There was something about him that was different.

He looked despondent, like their reunion in the warehouse never happened.

Sitting next to him, she whispered, "What are you doing awake?"

Kit didn't respond, and his silence brought about a rush of panic in her that she hadn't felt since she was last in his bedroom looking through his stuff. For a moment, she had to ponder what on earth could make him so emotionally vacant. Then it hit her. Grabbing the lamp, she contorted the metal arm towards his shoulder to be met with the worst possible scenario—a faint red cross.

Josephine's first reaction was to jump back. She'd seen plenty of these before in her life working with her kids, but the visual on someone she loved was something entirely different. It spoke to her, and what it was saying could not be any clearer — "Tick Tock Mutherfucker."

In what was the most depressing doctor's waiting room Josephine had ever visited, she and Kit sat in two boney, lino covered seats surrounded by peeling walls and outdated Nox Anima public awareness posters. The messaging on the posters couldn't have been more at odds with the smiling faces that adorned them. People hugging and laughing knowing they were going to die. It was bullshit and Josephine knew it. She looked down at her clothes and straightened them. She had made a half assed attempt to dress like Kit, borrowing one of his t-shirts. Again she felt like a poser, especially in an overworked, under resourced medical center like this where people toiled away from cheering crowds.

Kit, on the other hand, was not looking at anything—his body, gaze, even the energy he emitted was somber to the point of failure. He had won briefly but now was losing big time, actually more than any other Rat he knew. Although he didn't know who Icarus was, he was aware of the analogy of flying too close to the sun, and that was now him.

"Kit?"

The two of them looked up to be greeted by a worn-out doctor who looked to be in her late forties. She was the only thing that looked worse than the office. This woman was doing God's work and getting paid and treated like a leper. She nodded at them to follow her. As they entered her office, the doctor analyzed the couple and knew immediately that these two were breaking the law.

She gave an extra-long blink as if to say *When are these fucking kids going to learn?* But always the professional and adhering to the Hippocratic oath, she cleared her throat and attempted to erase any preconceived notions she had of these two. "So Kit what can I do for you?"

Josephine pounced. "We want to know what we can do so he can live longer?"

The doctor paused at Josephine before turning back to Kit. "When did your cross appear?"

Josephine couldn't help herself. "Yesterday."

The doctor lowered her clipboard, she had heard enough.

But Josephine hadn't finished. "The kids at my youth group use Axophrodine all the time."

The doctor humored her. "Do they?" Her tone

carried that blunt edge of life experience and sent Josephine retreating.

The doctor set her clipboard down on the counter and crossed her arms. It was time for the adult to speak now. "Right now, what you two are doing, is putting me in a position where I can lose my job for aiding an illegal couple."

Kit looked away, Josephine looked down.

"I've got a suggestion, stop putting stupid ideas into his head and I'll pretend you were never here. In five months time when shit really starts getting real, then and only then, I will see him and only him in my office."

Josephine kept her head down. It was a scolding she hadn't experienced since she was a sixth grader.. The doctor stood up and slammed the door leaving the two of them there to let themselves out.

Walking along the street, Josephine was charged from the verbal dressing down. Kit was ambling behind, the exchange had zapped him of any hope.

Josephine couldn't help but repeat the exchange in her head until she stopped and faced Kit. "Who the hell is that woman to tell me who I should and shouldn't love! She's barely part of the solution, people are still dying on her watch!"

Kit grabbed her arms gently, the opposite of temperaments. He tried to calm her down, but Josephine was ready to go ten rounds with that woman.

"Come on, this is not you, let's just reset. It's been a big twenty four hours."

Josephine looked at Kit. What on earth was he on about? She'd never seen him like this. "Yeah and it's going to be a quick six months if we don't do something"

Kit was showing a level of acceptance that made her worry. If this was to rub off on her then they would have no shot. This red cross, appearing on someone she loved, brought out the true activist in her, from somewhere deeper within. It wasn't so much about the people anymore—it was about one person. Her person.

She looked at Kit, his eyes hanging low and sad but also tinged with the look of someone who was just happy he had this time to be with her. But that wasn't enough for Josephine. She ripped her arms out of his grip.

"Where are you going to go?" Kit asked.

"To fix this" She tried to urge him with her sense of urgency.

Kit remained calm. "You can't, Josephine."

Josephine yelled back, "Says who?" She turned around and walked off.

Kit responded back softly, "Society."

Josephine knew more about Nox Anima than most, definitely more than most Clean Skins and probably more than most Rats who just attributed it to their lot in life. The one thing she had noticed in her time was that if Nox Anima's effects hit early, like some of the kids she had seen pass through her youth group, the first and only step was to buy them more time. Hence why she had suggested the Axophrodine to the doctor. It definitely wasn't a cure, but had shown promising signs in slowing down the take over of the mutation by at least a few months. The only problem was that it was expensive and only discounted to those under thirteen. Josephine knew she couldn't get it unless she had a script from a doctor, and the only one she knew was her father.

Later that day, Josephine visited her father for dinner. Whilst he sat at the table watching her prepare the food, he wondered why all of a sudden she seemed like her old self again—that was the despondent, semi estranged daughter. He assumed it had been over between her and Kit but didn't dare ask directly. There was no way she would open up to him anyway. He knew it just by the disaffected tone in her voice anytime he called. The conversations were short and anytime he did ask what was wrong in the broadest sense, she dismissed it to a busy college schedule.

Josephine turned from her food and looked at her dad. "I'm going to wash up."

Montgomery offered a smile.

Josephine quietly stepped along the upstairs hall-way. Her intention was to never go to the bathroom or wash her hands, but to steal a prescription pad that she had noticed whilst cleaning up the study months back. Deftly, she pushed the door open, but left the lights off. The sunlight streaming through the gaps in the windows was enough. Stalking around, she headed straight for the pile of documents that were to be thrown away. Opening the shoe box, she located the prescription pads. This time, the top sheet of the pad was different. It had fresh writing on it. Bringing it up to the light, she scanned the scribble—citalopram, escitalopram, fluoxetine, all anti depressant medication. For a split second, Josephine forgot about Kit, forgot about Nox Anima and realized that her father was still in his own world of hurt and she had forgotten to ask.

Montgomery's voice called from downstairs "Josephine, I think it's ready."

Staring at that prescription pad, she ripped off the back half of sheets and stuffed them into her pocket before returning it to the desk drawer. "Coming."

That night Josephine sat on Kit's bed. In her hand was a box of Axophrodine they had purchased from the chemist with the stolen script. From the bathroom, Kit projected out noises that made it clear that this stuff did not agree with him. Nan, who would have usually been asleep by this time of night, was awake. She listened to the wrenching sounds.

Kit stumbled in, wiped the vomit from his chin, his eyes half closed, he took a deep breath and looked to Josephine. "I don't think my body likes that stuff."

Josephine's grip on the box tightened, before she hurled it across the room as it crumpled on impact. "FUCK!!!"

That night Kit slept. In fact, since the mutation's effects had initiated, he was sleeping a lot more than a healthy person would. Josephine, on the other hand, couldn't get a wink in edgewise. If she wasn't thinking of how to extend Kit's time, she was thinking of how to cure the mutation—some bizarre, irrational hope had her scanning her entire life panning for clues, moments, things her father may have mentioned that could lead her to something nobody else had been able to solve in forty years.

But she always ended in the same panicked headspace. *If you don't face it now, he'll be gone and you will have missed it all.* Her inner voice was telling her, but against her better judgement, she suppressed that feeling and decided there was only one thing she could do.

Montgomery lay splayed on the couch, dead to the world in his lounge room. His memory bot played a scene from his life on the wall. From outside, faint clanging noises came from the garage, yet none of them were enough to wake him. In the garage, Josephine moved boxes, tins of paint, old tools, anything that was in the way of her getting to the Nox Anima machine Montgomery had engineered decades ago. Dragging it to the center of the garage, she whipped off the tarpaulin and stood in its presence. Immediately she felt something. Was it hope?

A few moments later a voice broke her concentration.

"I guess you two are back together."

She looked up to face her father. He was still waking himself up from his afternoon nap session. She looked tired, and her face screamed of someone who had been through the emotional wringer.

Josephine responded defiantly. "I don't care that he has Nox Anima, and neither should you."

Montgomery let her words sit, and for a second, even accepted them as he silently nodded his head. "Most people don't care. But it's the law. And you're breaking it."

Josephine lived for these conversations—she'd had a number of them on stage, at debates, panel discussions, lecture groups. "What do you think of this law? Do you think it's fair?"

Montgomery remained calm. "It's not my call."

Josephine couldn't stand when those who had power didn't step up. If she could do it, and she was an average college student, then why couldn't those who had real pull in the world?

"It is your call. You have the machine. You have the cure. So step up and do your job." Her voice boomed all over the garage.

Again, Montgomery, with his age and wisdom, knew this was a battle between youthful idealism and tired, jaded, life experience. "Is that all I am to you? A way to him?" Montgomery's pivot from the issue to the personal was expert. He knew his daughter was someone deeply in love for the first time and not thinking logically.

"Well you've been pretty useless as anything else up until now."

It was one of those comments that was at once both devastating and hilarious at how offensive it was. Montgomery let out a little *hmpf* sound. It was one of those moments where he realized he didn't know his daughter anymore.

Montgomery weighed his words carefully—the longer he did, the more worried Josephine became, her regret was instantaneous.

"I know you're mad, I also know you're in love, so let me be the most useful I can. Please put away that machine before you hurt not only yourself, but an innocent young man."

Josephine needed a moment, this theme of people

trying to protect her, Kit, her father, Elizabeth, even Don at her youth group, had become noticeable. She hated the fact that she was perceived as being a helpless young woman, mostly by men. Worse was the fact that they didn't recognize her understanding of Nox Anima and the work she had put in. "Why is everyone trying to protect me!!"

Montgomery barked back. "Because you don't know what you're getting into."

She could tell he was hiding something, information maybe. She knew her father and knew when he wasn't playing all his cards, but it didn't matter. Now both of them were yelling, the fight purely emotional. "You know how I know this is real? Because I *don't know* what I'm getting into. When was the last time you felt like that?"

Montgomery didn't answer right away, but he knew that Josephine knew there was only one answer—her mother.

Josephine didn't care, she steamrolled over his silence. "You see, you can't even remember, because you never risked it all." She began crying, the combination of her anger, the regret of things said and her lack of emotional stamina at this point had burst the damn wall. "I'm sorry dad, but I'm not leaving without that machine."

"And who's going to operate it?" His tone was blank, he figured this sobering reality would finally put this exchange to rest.

"You're not the only doctor out there."

Montgomery could see it in her eyes. She wasn't leaving without this machine. He lifted his hand off the console and took half a step back. Looking at his daughter, he thought to himself, *We only have each other and yet we ended up like this*? He offered her the saddest of smiles, a smile Josephine tried her hardest to deflect, before saying, "I guess you don't need me anymore."

Josephine gripped the console and wheeled it towards the open garage door. Both took one last look at each other as the garage door closed, a goodbye that neither had the stomach to say in person.

Sitting at Kit's desk, Josephine studied her father's machine. Kit remained asleep on his bed, just bringing the thing up the stairs had made him tired. A man who once could clear an entire apartment in a few hours with a few friends was now struggling with something the size of a small filing cabinet. Josephine dangled her finger over the black switch, the thing resembled a giant Nintendo Gameboy with its cream colored exterior and smooth edges. If she ever was to get any answers, this was the time.

She pressed the button, and nothing happened for a moment. She could tell it was functioning by the low whirring noise emitting from its core. Like a hard drive booting up, the machine began its computations before pushing up a rising screen that emerged from the thin gap on the top side of the console. A pleasant chime accompanied a bunch of text *Property of Montgomery Dun, Nox Anima Balancer Copyright 2007, in cooperation with SysteemaVanDeGroot Labs.*

Josephine sat back. It was unsettling seeing her father's name accompanied by a date prior to when she could really remember him. Everything about the color, graphics, even the way the screen flickered felt so old. She imagined all those people, lab assistants, researchers, engineers, programmers, coders and her father, sitting around, watching this machine boot up for the first time in 2007. So much hope, so much promise, the solution to the biggest killer the world has ever faced residing within this daggy, dated looking box.

This thing was more than just a piece of hardware programmed to cure Nox Anima. It was a time machine. Something that could help Josephine understand her father just a little bit better, say the things he never had the guts to say to her in person. Unfortunately, at that moment, her mind wasn't there.

On the touch screen, a *Begin* button pulsed gently. Josephine pressed it, the button disappeared and presented an overwhelming set of options. She scanned each one in vein hoping the next would be an option she would understand, but there wasn't anything that made sense or filled her with any confidence. In fact, the menu and the machine had made her feel infinitely worse about the situation. Where was the option on the screen entitled *Reverse Nox Anima* or *Cure Nox Anima* or *Balance Nox Anima*? There was none.

Josephine felt that sharp feeling in her gut. It was a loss of hope. Reaching over, she pressed the black switch sending the screen back into the slot and the machine into power down mode. Her dad was right.

Who on earth could operate this machine if the man who invented it couldn't get it to do what it was supposed to do?

Josephine slunk back to the bed. She pulled the sheets over her, and wrapped her arms around Kit. He reciprocated but didn't wake up. Josephine rested her head on his shoulder and started crying.

CHAPTER 23
HAVE YOU DONE THIS BEFORE?

Montgomery stumbled around his house. He was drunk, hadn't shaved and was back to being all rounded shoulders and five o'clock growth. It had been a few days since Josephine had broken into the house and taken away his life's work. Even though he never really thought about that machine anymore, he still felt its absence. It had defined him for so long. Then again, maybe it wasn't the absence of the machine he was feeling, but Josephine's absence from his orbit.

Gripping the walls, he made his way to the lounge room and collapsed on the couch. His drink spilt but he didn't care as he picked it up off the carpet. Pausing for a moment, he attempted to focus his thoughts. It took everything from him. He closed his eyes and took a deep breath. "Memory Bots play In News Tonight."

Opening his eyes again, he unfocused, his body relaxed and slumped back into the couch cushions. On the screen the intro song to a Sixty Minutes style show played.

A presenter walked towards the camera. Behind him in the studio was an image of a young looking Montgomery in a lab coat accompanied by the headline, *He did it!*

The presenter clasped his hands, a serious look on his face. "Just last week, the world got news that Nox Anima may have finally met its match. That match came in the name of Dr. Montgomery Dunn, a young man who has seemingly found a cure to the mutation that has gripped the world and unfortunately divided our population. Tonight we talk with Montgomery and get an inside look into just how he and his team did it."

Montgomery took a sip of his drink, his face burning dismissiveness directly at the fake earnestness coming from the journalist. It wasn't so much that he failed at curing Nox Anima that bothered him—he gave it his best shot and got closer than anyone—but it was the fallout from the failure that he could never shake. The overhyping, the fact that he had said yes to every media opportunity thrown his way. Never once did he think to stop them and tell them that this procedure may have worked once, yet needed more testing, that he was just a young kid who got lucky.

But, at that time, the world needed a savior and Montgomery was only more than happy to throw his hand up.

What scientist in his late twenties, on the verge of saving mankind, wouldn't do it?

The story cut to a shot of a young Montgomery sitting in a chair in a lab, clean shaven, upright posture, a confidence that comes when you're too dumb to quit. He sat there, nodding thoughtfully to the softball questions gently tossed to him by the journalist.

"So you're saying that that machine over there can cure Nox Anima?"

Montgomery's face lit up, a smile that had now been eroded by time and failure. "Theoretically yes. We're still in testing, but it has proven a few times now, that it can do what we have programmed it to do. I would say within the next six months, we will have solved the problem and have the cure ready to administer."

The journalist couldn't help but smile, it was part encouraging and part journalistic license. "There are a lot of people counting on this."

Montgomery was quick to answer this time. "That's why I want to get it right." He dead eyed the journalist. There was a seriousness in his expression this time. He stood up off the couch. Something in his young self had partially sobered him up.

The journalist shifted tone to match Montgomery's. "You stand to make a lot of money if this is successful."

The young Montgomery again dead eyed the journalist. Something in him wanted to be taken seriously.

He paused, there was something behind his eyes—this thing was more than money. "Not if I give it away for free."

The journalist took a moment. It came out of Montgomery so quickly, with such indifference, as if to say *Stuff it*. The journalist had seen some events in his lifetime and decided to use his best patronizing / not patronizing voice—the type of voice a parent used when they know the answer but they want their child to figure it out themselves. "You think you can do that?"

Young Montgomery didn't waver. The journalist was done pressing. He wasn't getting any scoop out of this guy.

Montgomery made it clear to him. "I have to. This is not about making money, I'm not about making money, I'm about being the difference."

Old Montgomery put down his drink. "Pause memory bot."

The memory bot paused and remained on the focused stare of his younger self. Old Montgomery had a moment with his younger self, and all he could think was, what a dumb, reckless kid. He grabbed his glass and hurled it at the wall. It obliterated on impact, whisky running down the image of his promising face.

The next morning, Josephine and Kit sat in the kitchen eating breakfast. It was quiet between the two, the most sprightly person in the apartment ironically was Nan. She pottered around, pouring them cups of tea that they drank slowly and silently.

Josephine stared long at Kit before asking him, "What do you want to do today?"

Kit breathed in deep. It was clearly tough to take in oxygen. "Whatever my body will let me do."

Josephine was quickly coming to the conclusion that getting Nox Anima later in life was worse than getting it early.

The bell of the apartment rang. Everyone looked to the door.

"Who could that be?" Nan wheeled herself over to the door and opened it to find Montgomery standing there, sober, clean shaven, and ready to make a difference.

Nan smiled at him. "Your daughter is inside, come on in."

As Montgomery walked in Josephine stood up, perplexed at how her father found her.

Montgomery beat her to it. "I built the machine with a geo tracker." He looked over at Kit who wasn't looking great—it was the first time in a long time he'd seen a Nox Anima sufferer at this late stage up close and it socked him right in the stomach, producing a look on his face that Josephine hadn't seen in a very long time. Empathy.

He reached into his pocket, and pulled out a vial of liquid. "I thought you might need this. It will fight the symptoms as his body aligns with the new frequency."

There was a long silence, an embarrassed silence.

"You found a doctor?"

Josephine shook her head. "Not really. Half the people don't believe the machine exists. The other half don't want to risk their careers, and the one person we did find… well let's just say they were a little weird." She referred to the kid who had balanced Kit's Nox Anima stamp months prior.

Montgomery nodded. "I figured as much." He wanted to say something else.

Everyone gave him the space to say it.

"I want to help, I want another chance."

Kit looked up. "I think we all do."

Each person smiled at one another, this collective agreement to tackle this thing had instantly galvanized them.

"So what do you need?" Josephine asked.

Montgomery blankly responded. "A cauliflower."

A few moments later the four of them sat down at the kitchen table. A halved cauliflower was in the middle of them. With a knife, Montgomery pointed to segments. Nan, Kit and Josephine watched attentively.

"What Nox Anima does is convince your organs to

fail at a rough predetermined date. It's those toxins released that activate your red cross, as you know. Usually this happens between ages twenty five to thirty. Now we can't change your DNA, but what we can do is replicate the frequency of the mutation that travels down this pathway." He ran the blade of the knife along an invisible line. "That's where I'll be programming something which is Nox Anima free, then we'll slip it back in there and mask the old Nox Anima frequency." He sat back inviting any questions.

"So it's basically yelling louder than the other guy?" Kit asked.

"Exactly. But there is one hurdle... everyone's frequency is unique."

Josephine leaned in. "Which means..."

Montgomery was about to respond but stopped himself. He needed another moment. He looked like he was thinking of something he wanted to share, but instead he took a long blink and returned to the topic. "Ah... yeah... so... If I get it wrong, or it doesn't sit perfectly within the path of the old impulse, your brain... could short circuit."

They all leaned back in their chairs away from the cauliflower as the grim alternative of this procedure took hold.

Montgomery looked at everyone. "There is one more thing."

"What?" Josephine answered back completely deflated.

Montgomery chuckled to himself.

Josephine hadn't seen that in years. She reeled back wondering what on earth her father was on.

"Ah… the machine doesn't actually work."

Josephine straightened up. "Say that again."

Montgomery rubbed his eyes. He was devastated. "The machine doesn't work. It's missing a component. A very specific component. To fashion that part costs a lot of money."

Kit cut right in. "How much money?"

At that moment nobody noticed Nan wheeling away.

Montgomery wanted to put this tactfully. "With all due respect, I don't think you have it."

Nan reemerged and dumped Kit's box right on the table. "Problem solved." She looked at everyone; she meant business.

Kit looked over to her, silently shaking his head.

"Technically, this is for me, is it not?"

Kit couldn't disagree.

"Then I will spend it on whatever I damn well want."

Montgomery reached over looking at Kit for permission. Kit nodded his head as if to say *I can't argue with that*. Reluctantly he opened the box and reached in before pulling out the retirement brochure. A silence fell upon the table. Josephine and Montgomery now understood the gravity of this box and its purpose.

Nan made a *pfft* sound. "You can throw that in the bin."

Montgomery grabbed the wad of cash—the sheer girth of it surprised him as if he was looking at an illicit roll of money from a mobster. He thumbed through it quickly. "This should be enough, I'm sure I can convince them to make it off the books."

Josephine put her arm around Kit and pulled him in for a hug. The four of them sat in silence.

Nan appeared unsatisfied. "Can I ask you something, Montgomery?"

"Of course."

"Have you done this before?"

Montgomery reflected for the shortest of moments. "Once," he answered softly.

"And did it work?" Nan asked back.

"Once," Montgomery said even softer. Putting the money back in the box, he closed the lid and stood up, just like a doctor would after giving a diagnosis of some rare operable condition. "Time obviously is not on our side, but I suggest you think this over, even if for the rest of the day, because once we go down this path, there is no going back."

Everyone on the table nodded.

"If you say yes, I'll go get the part made. You bring the balancer back to my house. I'll update it, do a few trial runs and then we'll have a go at the real thing." He went to see himself out but, before leaving, he turned around and faced everyone one last time. "There is every chance this will not work. But if it does, Kit, your life is going to change. Whether that's for the better, I don't know, but understand that you will be saying goodbye to a way of life and that's not going to be easy. It's not dealing with Nox Anima that's the tough part, it's understanding how to live without it." With those words of wisdom, he closed the door.

The three of them sat silently. Kit looked at all of them, tears in his eyes. A smile came across his face. His answer was clear—everyone came in for a hug.

CHAPTER 24
AM I DREAMING?

Montgomery yanked open the curtains in his office revealing a forest of vegetation on the other side. It was the first time he had opened these curtains in years. He had no desire to—the room had held no joy. Instantly, the space became peaceful, which was important, because Kit was lying on an operating table in the middle of it, feeling nervous. Grabbing a remote control, Montgomery turned on some music; the track was slow, melodic and ethereal, it was Enya.

Montgomery continued around the room. There was a focus on his face that was reminiscent of that look he had when being interviewed all those years ago. Josephine sat next to Kit on the bed, her hand clasped tightly. She wasn't letting go.

Walking over with a needle, Montgomery paused and looked them both in the eyes. "Now, this here is the antigen I was talking about the other day. Once I administer this, there is no going back, okay?" He waited for Kit.

Kit offered a silent yes.

Montgomery heeded the go ahead and pierced Kit's skin with the needle. Josephine winced, but Kit barely noticed it. Montgomery put away the needle and grabbed a cloth cap, every movement was deliberate, it was as much about procedure as it was about ceremony. He was holding someone's hand and helping them step through a portal, from one way of life to another. This wasn't mere surgery, it was a rebirth and he was not only the guide but the creator of a life after life. Gently he placed the cap on Kit's head, and Josephine fastened it around his chin. A full head of wires that resembled multicolored spaghetti protruded from the top as Montgomery plugged each wire into his machine. Each one clicked in with a satisfying snap. A schematic appeared on the touch screen. It was Kit's brain. Josephine took notice. It was the first time she had seen this machine in action and it had her transfixed.

Montgomery made a few clicks on the built-in flat touch keyboard embedded on the surface of the machine. The schematic of the brain zoomed in and revealed a pulse originating from a corner before sending out a jagged line across the rest of his brain tissue. This repeated every one and a half seconds to the measure, like sonar or an echo locator. A read out appeared on the screen, *ANTIGEN TAKING EFFECT.*

Montgomery breathed in; he steadied himself. "Let's see what key your brain likes to sing in."

He tapped again on the keyboard and another prompt appeared, *CONFORMING BRAIN IMPULSE INTO WAVE FORM.* The waveform of the brain's impulse appeared on screen in bold. The next one appeared again but slightly different, then at the next one, Montgomery swung the screen toward them. "See that pulsing line, that's the impulse that carries your mutation, that line, for you, is Nox Anima, and I'm going to replace it."

Kit looked at the jagged line, how could something so insidious, so brutal, so indifferent to human life be so simple and innocent as to be manifested into a squiggly white line.

Josephine looked at her father. She wasn't following. "How are you going to replace it?"

He pointed behind her. "Grab me that box."

Josephine spotted a black felt box, the type of box that would hold an expensive fountain pen. She opened it, revealing something that ironically looked like an expensive pen. It had the weight and ergonomics of a laser pen used to scan books at a library.

Montgomery gripped the laser pen with a level of reverence you'd reserve for a sentimental piece of jewelry. This pen, as sleek and clinical as it looked, told a story older than Kit and Josephine.

He looked back toward them. "I'm going to do it with this." Montgomery stood straight and steadied his heart rate, and swallowed a few pills. "Beta Blockers, they will slow my heart rate."

They watched as the medicine took hold and his slight hand tremor became dead still. Guiding the end of the pointers laser beam, he locked it in line with the waveform on screen. Suddenly Montgomery was born again.

Josephine watched him. Everything he was doing was new to her—every face, adjustment, look, speech, it was like she was meeting the person her father was, and in a better world, could have been, and it was inspiring.

Keeping his eyes on the screen, he moved his head just slightly to Josephine. "Remember my arm is not going to be much use after this. You'll have sixty seconds to match the impulses before the state of freeze is broken and we lose it forever."

Josephine nodded but none of her expression exuded any confidence. So many years working at a grass roots level trying to solve Nox Anima. Now here she was, about to possibly cure it with a few taps of a keyboard. It weirdly made her feel obsolete, like her time as an activist was wasted.

She looked over to Kit and rubbed his cheek, as he fell asleep. "I'll be right here when you wake up." She placed her hand on his chest as he drifted off.

Montgomery shared the moment too, something behind his eyes was unsure but he offered a confident nod to his daughter anyway. "Jo, I'm ready."

Josephine paused and looked at her father; it was the first time he had called her Jo. Montgomery wasn't in the mindset to notice or even care but the gesture meant a lot to her. It made her feel like they were finally on the same team.

Looking back to Kit, she smiled at him before she made her way to the keyboard, her hand rising from Kit's chest, that contact was now gone.

"This is good, he's slowing down, which means his impulses will too, which will make them easier to track." Montgomery took one last breath in before falling into a meditative state. As he did this, the impulses became less and less erratic, as if his temperament was controlling the state of Kit's brain waves. "Okay, nearly there. On my mark. It's coming. Another five seconds. Five, four, three, two, one, go."

Josephine hit the enter button on the keypad and the prompt *Begin Process* lit up on the screen. The machine began to produce all sorts of noises, it was something akin to an old school computer overheating. The lights from the cap flickered and traveled down the wires into the console. Josephine stood there not knowing what to do or where to focus her attention until she locked onto her father.

With his laser pointer, he began tracing the wave-form on the touch screen. His hand was rock steady as he glided the pen in concert with the frozen wave-form. He didn't make a noise. In fact it didn't sound like he was breathing. Josephine dared not move. The only thing that could be heard was the gentle music in the background. As Montgomery got closer to the end of the waveform, a slight tremor took hold, the sweat beads formed on his brow. Josephine could see he was near capacity.

Montgomery gritted his teeth as he put everything he could into keeping his arm steady yet fluid. As his hand reached the end, it faltered, collapsing under the fatigue as he dropped the laser pointer. "Stop!"

His yell prompted Josephine to slam the button as the machine powered down and the screen saved his recorded tracing of the waveform. Josephine looked to her father who staggered backwards, sweat covering his forehead. He rubbed his arm. The man was depleted.

Josephine turned to the screen. A reading blinked in and out: *SAVING IMPULSE IMPRESSION.*

Montgomery shook the lactic acid from his tracing arm. "Okay, now replace the old impulse with the new one, just like I showed you."

Josephine started tapping away on the keyboard—her motions weren't entirely confident, everything was being recalled from the crash course her father had given her. The screen spat out an update: *REPLACING IMPULSE IMPRESSION*, five, four, three, two, one."

The newly recorded impulse placed itself over Kit's old one. Montgomery sidled up next to Josephine and watched the process take place on the machine's touch screen. He leaned in, eyes moving back and forth, following the synthetically made impulse as it made itself at home over the old Nox Anima one.

Josephine looked at her father, but he didn't appear entirely convinced. "What do we do now?"

Without taking his eyes off the screen, he responded, "We wait."

She looked back at the screen, a countdown had begun with a percentage figure reading 99, slowly counting backwards, hitting 98.

"What's that?" Josephine asked.

Montgomery watched the figure count down. "That's the amount of Nox Anima is left in his body, or how much it thinks is left in the body."

It was finally hitting Josephine, they had done it. "So when that hits zero—"

Montgomery cut in. "Yep."

Josephine turned around and hugged him. Neither could remember the last time they hugged but both were never going to forget this one.

Montgomery's office was empty. The music had been paused and the only sound that could be heard were the chirping birds outside the window. Clouds parted making way for a gold light which blasted through and spotlighted Kit. It was strong enough to gently wake him up. Gingerly he rubbed his eyes. He remained lying down, and clearly he wasn't ready to sit up. Looking around the room, he finally got his bearings and uneasily hoisted himself onto his elbows. He leaned over and caught his shoulder. It had a giant square patch of gauze on it.

Slowly, he pivoted his legs until they were hanging over the medical bed, every impulse was telling him to go to the mirror. Pushing himself off, he stumbled forward, his legs felt light, almost hollow. He gripped the bed and took a few seconds to steady himself. Gradually, he willed his body to stand upright and plodded over to the floor-to-ceiling mirror in the corner of the room.

Standing himself in front of it, he studied his face. He didn't look any different. The effects of the operation and the painkillers had yet to wear off so he couldn't tell if he was supposed to feel different either. He'd assume the operation was a success so technically he should be Nox Anima free and back to full health but, at that moment, his body just felt tired and groggy. Catching his shoulder again, he twisted himself so the patch faced the mirror. Reaching up, he gently pinched the corner and started peeling it downwards on an angle, each centimeter revealing his skin and nothing more.

No blue stamp and no faint red cross until finally the patch was completely off revealing a clean shoulder… which meant only one thing, he was a true Clean Skin now. This wasn't a jammer or black market software overhaul. It was the real deal and he didn't know how to process it, every impulse told him he should be happy, ecstatic, but instead he was in awe and even a little bit scared, he thought to himself, *who is this guy in the mirror, he certainly isn't me, and how does he live his life now?*

He touched his shoulder, hoping maybe physical contact would provide him with some answers, but his mind just raced ahead at what his life was going to be and backwards at what it was. A creak from the other side of the room broke his stupor. It was Josephine. Her presence was gentle, as if any big movements or loud noises might activate the Nox Anima again. Her steps were slow and calm as she moved herself behind Kit and draped an arm over his shoulder.

Her head leaned into the crook of his neck.

Kit looked at her in the mirror "Am I dreaming?"

She offered him the proudest of looks, her eyes had become glassy, the tears a product of her bewilderment. She and her father had beaten Nox Anima, and now, she could spend the rest of her life with this guy. She rubbed his shoulder and looked back at him in the mirror, their eyes locked and the proudest of smiles took over her face. "No you're not. You're living."

CHAPTER 25
I DON'T KNOW THESE PEOPLE

Josephine and Kit stood inside an OurCloud clinic inside a shopping mall. It was sleek, clinical and designed of solely three materials—metal, timber and glass. The shopping mall itself was just another haven for Clean Skins, an extension of their life philosophy, spotless, airy, calm, and muted in tone. The natural light cascaded from the glass ceiling and bathed everyone in a warm wash. Being here was like getting a big soft hug.

A specialist, with a gentle face and glasses, strolled up to both of them and smiled. "Here to get an update?"

Josephine chimed in. "Actually no, someone needs an install."

The Specialist took a moment and gave Kit a once over.

Kit was starting to get used to it now in this new world.

"Okay, rare someone your age without an OurCloud, but I get it, good for you, nothing wrong with doing things old school." He waved them over to a couple of seats. and motioned for Kit to lay down in what was an ergonomic space aged recliner that was already in the reclined position. Sitting in his own brown leather chair, he took out a tablet and started tapping away. "Okay what is your name?"

Kit paused and looked over to Josephine who gave him a "go ahead" nod. "My name is Kitridge Dent."

The specialist expertly typed it in with one hand at a speed you'd see most people type with at two—a soft alert broke the waiting silence and he tried again. Seconds later, the same alert rang from the tablet causing the specialist to screw up his face. "That's unusual, there is no record of you anywhere." He looked up at both of them assuming they'd have an answer.

But neither of them did. They both just shifted in their chairs.

"Unfortunately if you're not registered, I'm afraid I cannot sell you an OurCloud account."

Now it was Josephine's turn to screw her face up. "Why not?"

The Specialist remained cordial. "Well for one, he would have no way of paying for it as there would be no record of the transaction." The more the Specialist sat with them the more doubtful he felt about the legitimacy of this couple.

Josephine pondered for a moment before a resolve came over her. She offered an expression that she usually saved for serious negotiations or rallying up a crowd. "So how important is this record of transaction?"

Forty five minutes later Josephine and Kit were walking out of the store. Both seemed pleased with themselves as if they had just executed a complicated scam. The specialist hung by the door. In his hands was a wad of cash. He thumbed through it immediately questioning his decision and his ethics. What did he just do?

Back at Kit's apartment, Josephine laid back on the bed, watching him with a bemused smile, like a parent watching their child take those first steps. Kit paced around the room, amping himself up like a prize fighter before a bout. Josephine couldn't shake the joy off her face.

"You got this, okay. Soon it's going to be part of you and you won't realize how you lived without it."

Kit nodded and sucked in a lungful of air. "Okay." He pressed the button behind his ear, and a screen projected out from his eye causing him to freeze.

Josephine couldn't help but blurt out a chuckle. "Just relax, you don't need to stand still, you're not trying to escape a T-Rex."

Kit just offered the most rigid of nods.

"Okay, now start slow and start sliding through your carousel."

Kit unlocked his posture and straightened himself up but kept one hand on the edge of his desk for balance as his projection screen remained. He stared it down. To him, this was something to conquer. If meeting Josephine was his introduction to the world of Clean Skins then mastering the OurCloud was his assimilation.

The frames began to slide to the left. His carousel presented a new frame after every swipe—one being a home screen another being a call screen. The flicking built speed until his carousel was spinning at a rate that no human could control.

Kit let out an anguished "Arghh!" and fell to the ground before buttoning off from his OurCloud.

Josephine laughed as Kit shook his head.

He had never struggled with anything in his life. He was built for most physical things but learning how to use this was beyond his day to day skills. "You know, it's not funny," he huffed.

Josephine covered her mouth. "I'm sorry, but it is a little."

Her smile softened him and he smiled back. He could see the humor in this moment but it was suddenly broken by his ringing phone. Both of them glanced over, his phone was buzzing and vibrating all over his desk.

"Who is it?" Josephine asked.

"It's Jim, I'll call him later."

It was a conversation both of them knew Kit was going to have to have at some point. The outcomes and emotions of the conversation were too much for Kit to handle at that moment. He wondered how he could break it to his best friend that he'd crossed over to the other side, and not in an illegal way either. He'd done it legitimately, with cutting edge science.

How would he broach this subject without offering the same cure to a man who had been by his side his entire life?

Surely Jim was as deserving of it as he was. Kit just happened to have fallen in love with the right woman. Or would he just keep this world changing procedure quiet, cut himself off from the community and the life that he knew, wait it out until all his friends were dead, which most of them were. If word got out, it would cause pandemonium in the streets. The simple fact of the matter that was starting to scare both of them was that Kit—a nobody from the Flats—had in one day, become ground zero as the first person to beat Nox Anima. It made Kit's head spin and Josephine truly worried at the fallout.

Weirdly the best outcome was one where Jim was happy for his friend but had no interest in the procedure. But that seemed wishful. The only other option was not to tell Jim at all and wait until he died. The phone continued to ring as if Jim was aware there was news to be divulged. Kit reached over and turned it off.

"Come on, I'll try again." Kit stood up and readied himself for another spin of the carousel.

The next morning, Jim walked towards his truck. He had a cigarette hanging from his mouth and looked like someone who was missing a significant piece to themselves, that piece that made him whole. Looking up, he spotted Kit leaning on his truck. He was not dressed like a Clean Skin but he certainly wasn't dressed like a Rat anymore. Jim stopped at the sight of him. "Why are you dressed like that?"

Kit didn't answer, he knew Jim knew that it only meant one thing, he was back with Josephine.

Jim strode to his truck, Kit as good as dead to him now.

"Jim," Kit was pleading but Jim had made up his mind.

This guy was well and truly dead to him. He'd given him enough chances.

"Jim, let me explain."

Jim opened the door to his truck.

Kit banged on the windows but they remained closed. "Jim! Jim!! Please!"

The starter motor rumbled as Jim kicked the truck into gear, burning away, forcing Kit to jump back from the driver's side window.

"JIM!"

Jim and the truck were well and truly gone. Jim glanced in the rear-view mirror, his last living buddy becoming visually insignificant, just like their lifelong friendship.

Kit pulled out his box from underneath his bed. That chunk of cash was now only a bunch of notes. The lack of heft he was so used to when holding that wad was now replaced with a sharp panic to his nervous system. There was no way he could go back to work. That was Jim's world now and he couldn't show his face there anymore.

Looking around the room, Kit surveyed what he owned—it was a wide variety of junk, stuff that could definitely be sold, but it was also stuff that defined him as a Rat for most of his young adult life. His first big screen TV, his first watch, a laptop, skateboards, sneakers—looking at it in totality made him question it for the first time and realize that he would give it all up to have his best friend back.

Later that day, he dumped a giant box of his possessions on the glass counter of one of his neighborhoods many pawn shops. He had a hopeful look on his face. It gave the impression you could offer him anything and he would take it.

The seen it all before Pawn Broker rifled through the goods and immediately pulled out the gold watch. After inspecting it, he offered it back to Kit. "You sure you want to part with this?"

Kit took it and read the back side of the watch. Engraved in simple clean font, it read: *Love you Kit, happy birthday, Mum and Dad.*

Kit took a beat, the watch acted like a time machine, guiding him back to the moment that watch was given to him, back to when his parents were alive, the last time he remembered being taken care of. He handed it back over. "What can you give me?"

A few days later, Josephine was holding Kit's hand as they took a tour of the university. For the first time, he wasn't an intruder on University grounds. It felt different being a guest. In front of them was a tour guide and in his hand a campus brochure. They stopped underneath a tree as old as the campus itself. The guide gave them a history of a particular blue stone building. Kit looked over to Josephine. She was beaming as she was mentally planning and piecing all the moments they were going to share together as students on this campus.

Kit was concerned and finally leaned in and whispered to her. "I can't afford any of this… I'm sorry I didn't tell you but I'm pretty much broke."

Josephine grabbed his hand. It was warm and calmed him right away. She turned back to the guide and asked, "Can you tell us about the Student Study allowance?"

Kit creased his face then turned to the tour guide who backtracked over her rehearsed speech. "Oh yeah, each student here gets a study allowance that is deposited into their OurCloud account every fortnight. It's based on your household income. The more your parents and you earn, the less you get, any questions?"

Kit had frozen, Josephine couldn't help but send a smile his way. Kit cleared his throat.

"No, thank you, that's great," she said out loud before whispering into his ear, "You're going to be okay."

Back at her dorm, Josephine sat on the bed, leafing through Kit's enrollment forms. She looked up to find Kit flicking through his OurCloud like a pro. She felt proud—proud that they saved their relationship but even prouder that she had given someone a new lease on life and access to the world, a world they were entitled to.

Kit turned to her and casually turned off his projection as if he'd been living with this thing his whole life. "I gotta go home, check on Nan. She hasn't been great recently."

Josephine shuffled over to him and rubbed his shoulder. "She's getting worse?"

Kit nodded. "Yeah."

Josephine handed him his papers. "Here you need to fill these out and we can return them when you come back. The one thing they keep in hard copy. You'll be good at that, doing things old school"

They kissed—it was the kiss of two people who needed nothing more in life now that they had each other on an infinite timeline.

"Okay I gotta go." He kissed her again.

Neither wanted to let go but finally they did and Kit jogged out of the room.

Moments later Kit was in the back of Josephine's self driving car. He passed through his side of town, the Rat side of town, the pawn shops, the gun shops, the liquor stores, the Rats getting harassed. None of it had changed but it now felt foreign. It wasn't his side of town anymore. It made him wonder, with Josephine in his life and a college education, what would he be now? More importantly, was he going to like what he was going to become?

The restaurant come bar was at the forefront of Clean Skin cool. Again like the Clean Skin community itself, the interior, the food, the music and the vibe were just an extension of the people who frequented this place. Josephine, Kit, Elizabeth and ten of their friends held court at a large rectangular table. The restaurant was busy and they were the center of that busyness which made them all feel like the center of the world, or at least their world. Kit and Josephine had decided not to tell anyone that Kit was now Nox Anima free. The love bubble they were in was too comforting to pop right now.

Everyone had ordered some version of a vegetarian meal, except Kit who had stayed true to his carnivore roots. Josephine sat at one end and was in the depths of a conversation with a friend, whilst Elizabeth sat across from Kit and watched him masticate the dead calf with a look that could only be described as contempt coupled with the slightest bit of curiosity. It took Kit a moment to realize that he was being watched.

Elizabeth offered him a fake smile but it was solely to make him feel even more self conscious. Kit slowed his chewing down and looked over at Josephine but she was thirty minutes deep into a conversation that looked to have no end.

Elizabeth craned her head into Kit's line of sight in an attempt to get him to look at her again. "You know, I've been watching you this evening, at this restaurant, with *my friends* and I just can't work it out. How did you manage to snake yourself into our world? You know if it was anyone else I would drop the bomb immediately and tell everyone not to get too comfortable with you, but I love my friend too much so I'm going to say this as nicely as possible… you're going to be dead soon."

Kit stopped chewing, it took him a moment. *Did she just say that?* Calmly he put down his knife and fork and finished what was in his mouth. His face slowly turned blank before turning to stone. It was a stare only reserved for when he and Jim had to throw down back in the day, a look no Clean Skin would have ever encountered because their world never required it.

Elizabeth swallowed hard and began shifting in her seat. Quickly she avoided eye contact and started searching the table for other conversations but his ice-cold glare had locked her in and she couldn't escape.

Suddenly a familiar tune, in fact the world's most familiar tune, broke the standoff. Happy Birthday rung out amongst the table; the entire restaurant halted as diners usually do when it was someone's birthday. Kit looked around as a cake and its dazzling sparkler candles were placed in front of him. Elizabeth looked as perplexed as Kit did. He was trying his best to shift gears and shed that simmering fury that had consumed him only moments ago. The table continued singing, all of it led by Josephine.

Moving over, she crouched down over his shoulder and kissed him on the lips. Looking directly into his eyes, she was unaware of the tension between him and her best friend, all that she had on her mind was "Happy 28th birthday!"

Kit smiled but it masked a growing anxiety. Everyone was waiting for him to say something but he couldn't. His chest grew tighter and tighter, his face paler, even Elizabeth began to look concerned until finally he couldn't handle it anymore and busted away from the table.

The door slammed wildly as Kit charged into the bathroom like a bull. He paced the tiled white floor hoping to calm himself down but his movements only added to the growing tightness in his chest.

Josephine peeked her head inside before closing the door behind her. "What's wrong?" A look of genuine concern was on her face.

Kit breathed in deep a few more times, it finally seemed to be working. "What the hell was that?"

It took Josephine a moment. "What? Your birthday?"

Kit nodded.

Josephine stammered, she was still shocked by the reaction. "I just thought we'd celebrate it."

Kit shook his head. "With them?"

"They're our friends."

Kit was finally thinking clearly and had managed to steady his heart rate. "They're your friends. I don't know those damn people. What history have I got with them?"

Josephine put her arms around Kit in a bid to settle him down. "I know your life has changed."

Kit felt offended by the word "changed." It seemed like a gross understatement, but it also made him feel like an ingrate because this woman had given him new life. But he said it anyway, "I think changed is an understatement, Josephine, I should be dead, doesn't matter how hard I try, I can't shake that feeling."

There was a pause as Josephine tried to empathize with his situation. "Maybe we have to take this a little slower. I got carried away because we have the luxury to get carried away now."

"I just need more time." He hugged her, before she pulled away and looked to him.

Twinkle in her eye, her mind ticking over, she said to him softly, "I have an idea."

Later that night in a fast food restaurant on the Rat side of town, Josephine and Kit sat in a booth. Surrounded by burgers, nuggets, thick shakes and fries, the two of them scoffed down the greasy goodness. It was the second time Josephine had eaten this stuff and was beginning to think it could be a permanent fixture. Kit looked at her, finally he recognized how amazing this woman really was, and she had chosen him. How?

They stopped chewing and stared at each other. With food in their mouths, they kissed, its sloppiness eliciting a laugh from both of them.

"Happy birthday," Josephine said.

CHAPTER 26
YOU KNEW

A month later, Josephine and Kit sat in Montgomery's kitchen eating dinner. Josephine and Kit were in their own world. They chatted and ribbed on each other as if the last nine months never happened, as if Nox Anima never existed and it was never a thing between them. They were now just a couple of kids who met in an ordinary time, where loving someone was a simple as giving yourself over to them wholly.

Across from the table sat Montgomery. He played with his napkin. He looked despondent, but not in an alarming way, but his mind appeared elsewhere, one eye scouring the past and the other scanning the future. He was still struggling with what was sitting in front of him.

Did he just complete his life's work? Did he just solve the greatest plague of the twenty-first century? And if so, what the hell would he do now? He struggled with the implications. It would be immoral not to make this news public. Then again, it worked only once before back in the day. What happened if it didn't work again, and what happened if it was made public knowledge? Imagine the civil unrest it would cause.

If this had happened when it was supposed to happen, when he was young, it wouldn't have been a problem. The young Montgomery was never this much in his head. The young Montgomery knew it was his destiny to cure Nox Anima. The young Montgomery had a motto. *Move fast and break things.*

"Dad, you okay?" Josephine asked.

Montgomery gave them a slow, calm silent nod. "I was thinking, what are you two going to do about this in six months time?"

They were so in love they hadn't thought about the fallout if the two of them had gone public. Well, at least not enough to have come up with a strategy. Josephine thought about it for a moment. It made her uncomfortable and even a little embarrassed that she had forgotten. Or maybe she was finally just thinking of herself for once, stepping out of her masculine energy and getting to enjoy her feminine energy for the first time, instead of being the driver, the motivator, the caretaker, now she got to fill her own cup.

Montgomery was waiting for their answer.

Kit didn't have one. Weirdly, he felt like he shouldn't need one. He was the guinea pig and, like for most of his life, only thought about the future in terms of his Nan. "Do we have to tell people?" Kit's answer was slow to slide out.

Josephine was somewhat surprised. His answer was selfish but she herself didn't have a better one.

Montgomery gave the lightest of chuckles, the type of response where you realize you may be screwed. "None of us really thought about this did we?"

All three remained silent, mentally recounting past conversations to see if any thought or suggestion had been thrown up, but it hadn't, and now it was time to pay the piper.

Montgomery drew in a big breath. "Why don't we sleep on it, we don't need an answer now but we do need to start formulating a game plan because whatever we do, it's going to come back at us from all angles and you two are going to have to be ready."

The two of them nodded. It felt like a stay of execution.

Montgomery stood. "I'll see you guys tomorrow morning. We can do your check up then, Kit. Goodnight."

Both Kit and Josephine responded in unison. "Goodnight"

In Josephine's old bedroom, Kit lay on the bed contemplating. "Why does this now feel harder then when I had Nox Anima?"

Josephine shared the same mindset. Her eyes stared blankly at the wall as she sat next to Kit. She wanted to keep it positive. They had gone through hell to get here, no way were they going to let this be the toughest test of their love. "It's not harder, Kit. It's just different."

Kit let out a noise that reflected that he wasn't entirely sure.

Josephine looked to him and projected back a smile. "Hey you know what we haven't done?"

Kit had no idea.

"We need to fill your bio out for your OurCloud page."

Kit shrugged. "I have no idea what to write. I can't write the truth right, at least not right now."

Josephine thought it over. She had managed to pull him away from the unease he felt about his life becoming public knowledge and wanted to keep it that way. "You know what, it's always best to start with a photo with these things."

Josephine laid next to Kit and for a second the two said nothing. They just stared at each other and enjoyed the silence and closing of space between their faces. They kissed for a little bit before pulling away and looking at each other again. It made them forget that there was a whole new chapter of this relationship that they would have to navigate. Nestling her head into the crook of his neck, she pressed his cloud button behind his ear. His projection popped up.

"Okay now all you gotta do is command your cloud to take a photo and then blink your eyes."

Kit nodded. "Seems easy enough… OurCloud take photo."

The screen wiped and produced an image looking outward.

Reverse camera—the image flipped to reveal both of them lying on the bed.

"That's us," Josephine said, her voice bolstered with a sense of pride.

It was contagious and made Kit smile. "Yeah, it is… okay, you ready, because this is going to be my profile pic."

Josephine maneuvered herself to get the best angle. "I'm ready."

Kit counted down. "Three, two, one." He blinked and the projection produced a click and flash similar to that of a real camera.

What was frozen was the two of them, smiling, looking at whoever was looking back at them and saying, "This, us, we are forever."

The next morning, Josephine woke before Kit. This was unusual but Kit had trouble getting to sleep that night. The dilemma posed to them by Montgomery had Kit longing for simpler times. He was sleeping on his side, his well-toned back acting like a wall blocking Josephine from any chance of seeing his face. As if reading her mind, he rolled onto his back.

For a second, it didn't register; she was so in love with this man her eyes went directly to his face. She scanned his nose, his stubble, his shaved head and his lips.

There were so many things about this guy she was in love with, but seconds later, it hit her, a reaction so visceral, she jerked violently backwards. Her face immediately drained of any life, she didn't dare move, everything in her world had gone quiet. The edges of her vision had gone dark forcing her to focus on one thing and one thing only—Kit's red cross. It had returned.

Josephine reached out to touch it and accidentally woke him up. She was too scared to be in the bed with him so jumped out and hugged the wall. She couldn't act natural, that Red Cross had rendered her speechless. Slowly Kit stirred before finally rising, leaning on his arms he turned toward her. He was still half asleep but the expression on Josephine's face woke him up quick smart.

"Hey, you okay?"

Josephine began crying, tears silently rolled down her cheeks.

"What's going on?" He scrambled out of bed and quickly closed the space between them. He put his hands over her arms. "Josephine talk to me."

She couldn't mutter anything but a gentle sob. Gradually she stepped away to her right revealing the body length mirror. There Kit stood half naked, only in a pair of boxer shorts, the edge of the cross was visible even from a front angle. He slowly turned his shoulder flush towards his reflection. Kit stared at it. There it was, more prominent than ever now that Kit had no stamping ring.

"Kit," Josephine pleaded with him softly.

He didn't hear her, his face was a mess of every emotion. His first impulse was to punch the mirror, but instead he backed away. He didn't get far; his legs gave out. "Urgh." He tumbled backwards over the bed.

It was the first time Josephine had seen him so ungraceful, so not in control of his body. Kit hoisted himself up on all fours and started searching, the moment was overwhelming him and he needed an out.

"Let's just stay calm," Josephine begged.

But he stood up without even the slightest recognition of Josephine's presence. Hurriedly he moved his way to the seat and started dressing himself.

"Say something," Josephine's voice started breaking. She went to touch him and he spun around lightning quick.

His gaze was uneasy and accusatory. He didn't have to say it but this was her fault or at least that was how he felt.

He stormed down the hallway, his footsteps thunderous. He charged towards Montgomery's bedroom. Josephine pleaded with him to stop.

SMASH! He bulldozed through the door and crashed into Montgomery's room to find him already awake and attempting to stand his ground. Kit rag dolled his middle aged body and smashed it against the wall temporarily winding him. "What did you do to me!!"

Josephine was hysterical. Through her wailing and tears, she attempted to pull Kit off of her father but he was stronger than the two of them combined. His sturdy Rat body was built for physical confrontations like this.

Josephine cried out again, "Let him go!"

Kit continued to slam Montgomery against the wall. Montgomery was still conscious but limp. He knew it was better to play half dead and let this man exorcise his rage.

"Tell me. What did you do to me?" Kit raised his fist.

Montgomery closed his eyes bracing for what would surely knock him out.

Kit launched his fist and punched the wall next to his head repeatedly. "How could you do this?"

BANG! BANG! BANG!

His fist destroyed the plastered wall and spat chips onto Montgomery's face. SLAP, like a circuit breaker Kit dropped Montgomery and staggered back holding his cheek. Josephine stood there as surprised as anyone that she had to hit Kit for the second time in their relationship. Montgomery lay on the floor, shaking from the ordeal. Josephine threw herself over her father sobbing into his arms.

Kit stumbled around; his eyes rolled into the back of his head until THUD. He passed out on the carpet.

An hour later, Kit was back to sitting on the medical bed in Montgomery's office. Everyone had calmed down, or more likely come to accept what had happened. The skull cap hugged Kit's head, the wires ran out of it and fed critical data to the Nox Anima console. Montgomery tapped away on the keys whilst Josephine stood meters away, her gaze down at the ground, her mind racing through the key moments in their relationship. Finally she looked up and for the first time she didn't see her boyfriend, the guy she was prepared to spend the rest of her life with, a guy who challenged her. She saw a man, with the most hopeless expression on his face wearing a cap with wires sticking out of it, a science experiment and it made her hate herself.

The screen zoned in on a schematic of Kit's brain and then further focused on the impulse. The impulse repeated again and again bringing with it a set of vitals. Under the heading Nox Anima, it blinked *Carrying*.

Montgomery took a moment. He closed his eyes for the longest of times before leaning back and taking off his glasses. There was no surer sign of someone ready to admit they screwed up. "There was a possibility of this happening."

Josephine turned to her father, her mouth agape. Kit had heard enough. Frankly he'd had enough of these people and this house. Unhooking himself from the machinery, he calmly placed the cap on the seat and lowered himself off the medical bed without the slightest of fanfare.

Josephine went to grab his arm. She spun him around. But he met her with a dead stare, his eyes vacant, like a veteran back from war struggling with the atrocities he witnessed. He wasn't angry anymore, he was destroyed. She tried to kiss him but he offered back nothing. He slowly extracted himself from her grasp and walked away.

Josephine started crying before turning her attention to her father who stood next to the machine not moving in a bid to avoid having her launch a tirade at him. Josephine wiped the tears from her eyes, she stared down her father, just like she did when she was taking the machine from him. "You knew." She was now resolute, she wasn't coming out of here without some form of contrition from him.

Montgomery's response wasn't at all empathetic. He figured he'd play the scientist once again, not the father. "I told you there was a risk."

Josephine's blood boiled, viciously simmering under

the surface until "*fix it*" screamed from deep inside her.

Montgomery tried to keep the situation calm,."I can't."

Josephine expected more, but her father had nothing, no empathy, just science.

She launched herself at him. "This is your fault! You did this. You knew." She threw her arms at her father's chest.

Montgomery stood there taking the punishment as Josephine beat down on him, her waifish Clean Skin physique fatigued easily leaving her to fall into his arms in a crumpled heap crying.

Montgomery grabbed his daughter and brought her in for a bear hug. She sobbed violently in his clenches which in turn made him cry. Tears ran silently down his face as the two of them realized the extent of what they had done to Kit.

CHAPTER 27
YOU TRIED TO FIX HIM

Kit entered his apartment to the comforting sound of the pottery wheel, except this time, it wasn't comforting. It didn't make him feel anything. He was too empty inside. He stood there in the middle of the lounge room watching his Nan work the clay. Somehow, like she always did, she sensed his presence amidst the noise and looked up to find him a shell of himself. Turning off the pottery machine, she wheeled over and put a hand on his arm. The touch sent him into a breakdown as he fell to his knees and started sobbing into Nan's shoulder.

A few days later, Kit struggled his way down to the carpark of the housing towers. It was a cold and frosty morning. He looked like he hadn't slept in days and the Nox Anima was starting to eat away at his physique a little bit. He was dressed in his work wear, his red cross now quite visible from under his sleeve. He walked to the truck, were Jim packed the trailer. Jim paused. He could weirdly hear the silence of Kit standing behind him. Kit stood there waiting, not making a sound but vibrating for forgiveness. Seconds later, a packet of gloves hit Kit in the chest. Jim still hadn't made eye contact.

He hoisted himself into his truck and said, "You can make your own way there." He started the engine, and ripped away leaving Kit to be grateful to breathe in his carbon monoxide.

It took about a week before Josephine had had enough. The hunger to go out there and fight for rights and help kids was well and truly gone. It paled in comparison to the highs she felt with Kit but also made her take stock of the bubble she lived in. An open suitcase sat on her bed. She tossed clothes in without a thought if they were going to fit or not. She was not going on a holiday, she was running away. Elizabeth walked in and asked this exact same question. Josephine didn't answer. There was a shame that hung over her. It would never happen but there was a small part of her that wondered if Kit had grounds to press charges.

What was the precedent giving someone hope then taking it away, even if it was on the grounds of love?

Elizabeth leaned against the door. "Where are you going to stay?"

Josephine continued to pack.

Elizabeth tried to get in the way of her line of sight before giving up and just gripping her by the arms and blocking her frenzied back and forth. She locked their eyes together. "You did a good thing. You tried to fix him, nobody in the world would have bothered to do that for him, or any one of those Rats."

Josephine yanked her arms away. "He didn't need fixing."

Elizabeth took Josephine's tone personally, since it was the first time Josephine had ever been mad at her.

"I can't do this anymore. I can't be here. It's all bullshit and I'm full of shit for believing it." Josephine slammed her suitcase close and left.

Elizabeth looked around. She couldn't help but feel abandoned now.

Josephine strode with purpose along the catwalk that connected all the apartments, reaching Kit's, she lifted a fist ready to bang on the chipped timber door. Instead she stopped short when she saw that the door was ajar. When she tapped it open, a familiar sound escaped. It was the pottery wheel.

She called out, "Kit!" but nothing but the continuing sound of the pottery wheel responded. Carefully she stepped inside. There was something else. The rhythm of the wheel was too constant, lacking in that randomness you get when someone interacts with it. Josephine walked over to the kitchen. She was shocked to see the entire area a chaotic mess of dishes, bottles and half opened rubbish bags. The noise of the wheel beckoned her to keep looking.

"Kit?"

Still she got nothing back. As she moved towards the lounge room, the sound of the wheel grew louder but not any different. When she edged around the corner her eyes met the wheel immediately. Below that, on the ground, two hands where caked in dry clay. It was Nan, she was on the floor, eyes open, slowly breathing to conserve her breath.

Josephine skidded to her knees and cradled Nan's head. "Nan can you hear me?"

Nan locked eyes with Josephine as she tried to goad more information out of her.

"What happened?"

Nan was still disoriented and looked around again trying to piece it all together.

"I fell over, Gem, is that you?"

"No, I'm Josephine, Jo, Kit's girlfriend, remember me?"

Nan's eyes began twitching, giving the appearance of a computer rebooting, like a torrent it flooded back bringing with it a return of coherence. "Oh that's right, the Clean Skin."

Josephine breathed a sigh of relief. "Yeah, that's me." Josephine smelt the air, she had missed the odor in the adrenaline of the moment. Looking down below Nan, she noticed a patch. The poor woman had wet herself.

Josephine sat Nan in her chair. "Do you need anything?"

Nan shook her head softly and gave her the quietest, "No, thank you."

There was no way she was going to let her sit there in her own piss. "No, let's fix this."

Josephine went about bringing order back to the house. It was her half attempt to create some clean and productive environment for Kit to come back to. She cleaned Nan in the bathroom. It was the first time she had to do anything of this sort. It was physically humbling, she never had to use these muscles before—lifting someone, lowering them, lifting them again. Nan was dead weight.

Josephine took a moment and stood back wiping the sweat off her brow. "Sorry, it's just…" She let out an exhausted sigh.

Nan looked at her gratefully but also with the slightest of bemused smiles. She was making an effort but seeing a Clean Skin sweat never got old.

After setting Nan back down in her chair and making her a cup of tea, Josephine went about cleaning the kitchen, and the half open pizza boxes, Chinese take away containers, the typical diet of a Rat but consumed by someone who was clearly eating their feelings. Next Josephine went about scrubbing the pee off the rug.

Nan watched her from her wheelchair. "You know you don't have to do that."

"If I don't, who will?" She kept scrubbing. Finally she took a break and sat at the kitchen table where only a few months ago, they had discussed and solved the biggest problem to plague modern man. Josephine looked at the steam rising from her cup. It evaporated and reminded her of how things could disappear so quickly in life—without any concern for your feelings or your plans.

I guess that's what you get for trying to capture hope, she thought.

Nan wheeled in and silently settled across from her, offering that smile again. "You tried, it's not your fault. You're young and it's okay to feel like this. Trust me it will pass."

It didn't make Josephine feel any better.

Nan instead pivoted to something a little lighter. "You look like your father. Did anyone ever tell you that?"

Josephine shook her head. "Looking like him isn't enough these days. I messed up."

Nan shook her head. "No. You did exactly what you had to in the time you were given. Reminds me of my husband. He died young."

Josephine pondered for a bit, casting her mind back to a time that seemed unimaginable, a time pre Nox Anima. "What was it like back then? I mean life, I mean I know from like books and study, but what was it like for you?"

Now Nan cast her mind back, it brought a cheeky chuckle. "Racism, Sexism, but you didn't need to build your life around a number, you built it around a person, around their character. And sometimes that life you built was taken away from you a little early, but that's the price you pay. Doesn't seem like anyone wants to pay that price anymore, because we have a Red Cross and Blue Light that does it for us now. So tell me Josephine, are either of you ready to pay the price?" Nan reached for her bottle of medication and downed a few more pills than usual.

Kit was used to eating lunch alone now. His chewing was slow, as if eating was only serving the purpose of sustaining him and nothing else. A few meters away sat Jim and the rest of the removalist crew. They jibed and jockeyed whilst the radio played from Jim's truck which had the passenger side opened.

Jim snuck a look at his former best friend. It struck him in the chest, that loneliness he was feeling now. Jim had lost once, but Kit had lost thrice in this life—first Gem, then Jim and now Josephine. As shitty as a friend he had been, nobody deserved that. A Rat's love life was hard enough. Still Jim didn't do anything. Right at that moment, Kit looked up and spotted Jim looking at him. Neither of them changed their expression, but neither of them offered anything to say that it was over. They both thought the same thing right at that moment: Baby steps.

Yet it wasn't enough to stop Kit from going to the strip club later that afternoon. He drank what he could afford and stumbled around the place haphazardly trying to dodge the haze and the criss cross lights. Leaning on a wall, he fell into a funk. He looked around. This wasn't where he wanted to be. A "fear of missing out" twigged inside him—those eighty plus years that Josephine was going to live without him, the nights out, the get togethers, the nights on the couch, rainy days looking at each other in silence, running his hands through her hair, her running her hands over his chest, the laughs, the road trips, the fights, the make ups and the sex. It created this weird feeling of longing, back to when he would glimpse her mentoring the youth group and wondered how he could be a part of her life. It was too much for him to bear.

He shook himself out of it and focused his view on a dancer that from a distance resembled Josephine. It wasn't her of course, but if Josephine had gotten breast and butt implants and blanketed herself in tattoos, they could pass as sisters. Kit staggered towards her whilst doing his best sober impression. As he bumped into the stage, she looked at his sad face and knew she had a live one.

Kneeling down to him, she touched his face. "You look sad," she said in the most empathetic of voices, a voice she had used countless times before. Stepping off the stage, she grabbed Kit's hand and whispered into his ear, "I can fix that."

The youth center was cold and dark without the chaotic overlapping chatter of the kids. It looked miserable and uninviting, let alone a place where kids went to forget their troubles and get free food. The door creaked open revealing a five inch sliver of light and the silhouette of Josephine. She stepped in and stood right in the center. Without her kids, this place felt as foreign as the housing towers. Making her way to a supply cupboard, she pulled out a couple of foam gym mats and a dirty blanket. Settling herself into a corner, she laid herself down, the smell of the old gym mats soon became bearable and she fell asleep. It had been a long day, actually it had been a long year.

Montgomery stumbled through his home, although it didn't really feel like a home anymore, just a museum of his failures as a doctor and parent. A bottle of gin followed him around as he gripped it loosely by the neck. The lights were off because he felt more comfortable in the dark. He couldn't bare to look at himself when he passed a mirror. If he spent the remainder of his days existing in the shadows, that would suit him fine.

He worked his way through his house, up the stairs, down the hall way and into his office. He kicked open the door. The moonlight streamed through the windows and bounced off the greenery outside. Montgomery looked around at what was left of his life's work, the machine, the medical bed, papers and books still remained, all of it mocking him. Just a man who tried and failed and ultimately destroyed a lot of people's lives along the way.

In the last few years, he began to long for a normal life—one where he didn't discover Nox Anima, one where he took over the family farm instead and lived a simple existence tending to cows and sheep. It was never the life for him, it was too basic, it was the thing he had always been afraid of, being ordinary.

Moments later, Montgomery was arm swiping documents and books into large plastic bags. He grabbed his laptop, and tossed it into the bag without concern about its delicate internal components. It slammed to the bottom with a cringey thunk. He looked around, and decided he wasn't finished. There was still the Nox

Anima machine, all of his grandest ambitions and insecurities summed up in a dumb box. He walked towards it with a menacing limp. Lifting his leg, he nudged it; it balanced on a corner before tipping back. He tried it again, this time pushing with enough force to get the result he wanted. Bang. It hit the ground with all its top heaviness contacting the floorboards with dull force.

Montgomery stood over it. Lifting his leg again, he was ready to throw down, but something stopped him. He noticed a face within the buttons and dials. It wasn't on purpose—it was simply a by-product of its design, a happy accident, the face looked back at him and pleaded, "Please don't, I still have value."

Montgomery gradually pulled his foot away and set it down.

Outside in his backyard, a shudder inducing screech bellowed out amongst the neighborhood. The noise was the sound of a metal drum being dragged, the metal on concrete produced sparks. Montgomery shimmied the barrel left and right until he had it exactly where he wanted it. He grabbed the garbage bags, and tipped their contents in. One by one they expelled their insides. Decades of knowledge and equations and nearly there's, was now thrown together inelegantly inside a drum. He pulled a swig from his bottle of gin, then doused a generous amount into the drum before lighting a match and tossing it inside—woosh.

His life work plumed into a fantastic flame that reached into the sky before settling into a manageable fire. Montgomery stood there for a while, his eyes glassy. He looked at the smoke climbing from the drum. It disappeared into the night sky and so did those things that made him who he was. A distant siren cut the peace. He was not concerned. It was most likely the neighborhood patrol car. Within minutes, two uniformed men emerged and approached Montgomery with some amount of trepidation. A bonfire in the backyard was the biggest call out these men had encountered in months.

"Excuse me sir."

Montgomery was hypnotized by the fire. There was a bond between him and what it represented.

"Sir."

Montgomery looked over and it was clear to them he was not doing well.

"Ah sir, it's against the law to burn anything that is not garbage."

Montgomery chuckled, as if these two men should already know the answer. "Pfft… it is garbage."

CHAPTER 28
BECAUSE IT DID...
ONCE

The morning hit through the dirty windows of the hall. The light touched Josephine's face causing her to bolt upright. Assuming she was still in her dorm, it took her a few beats to come to the realization she was not. She looked down at the gym mat that was her bed and her dirty blanket and breathed out. She sat there and looked around, but didn't know what to do. This image she had created of herself as the rebel and activist fighting the system didn't make sense to her anymore.

Was she really making a difference or just trying to absolve herself of some Clean Skin guilt?

It was something that didn't sit right with her anymore. Being with Kit was the realest she had ever felt. Maybe it was simpler than that, the highs she got from protests and activism didn't compare to the highs she felt being in love. The thrill she got learning about him, about herself, about other people. It didn't feel like theory like her college life, it felt like true growth, something that only comes from experiencing the best and worst of life.

Kit arrived at his apartment. He wasn't drunk but he wasn't completely sober either, but what couldn't be truer was that he hated himself or more accurately he hated what he offered to the world. Walking in, he was surprised to see the house clean. He paused for a moment, the vision of a tidy apartment sobered him up. Walking over to the fridge he stopped and looked again, hoping an answer would make itself present. He called for his Nan but got nothing back but also thought nothing of it, especially now the apartment was clean. Reaching into the fridge, he pulled out a can of whipped cream and gunned what was left of it before tossing it into the bin.

On the other side of town the door to Montgomery's house clicked open, the morning light cut through the main entrance. Josephine stumbled in looking like she had run all the way from the youth center. Even for her father, this place was dark, but then again it perfectly reflected her father's current state of mind. She stepped forward before pausing and tilting her ear towards the hallway where those sounds that had defined her father's latter years became clearer, dropping her shoulders she slunk her way to the lounge room.

Looking inside the bin, Kit spotted the prescription bottle sitting on top of the rest of the garbage. Grabbing it, he assumed the usual. Nan didn't take her pills, but when he lifted it, he noticed its lightness, its lack of weight. The clacking sound of shaking pills was not present. Most of the pills were gone and in fact the bottle wasn't even for her Alzheimer's, it was Temazepam, "For aiding sleep."

Josephine followed the chatter, a mother talking and young girls laughing. She knew the voices but couldn't recall the memory. She rounded the corner and edging towards the doorway she clocked her father on the couch. The man had hit rock bottom, food around him, empty bottles. He was too drunk to do anything but lay sprawled out, semi-conscious with one eye open, lucidly watching his memories. Josephine stepped inside the lounge room but her father was too inebriated to notice. She watched on, the memories playing from the bot were so real—her mother watching on as Josephine's twin sister twirled around a garden setting. Josephine's mother looked back at her through the projection, and for the first time since she could remember, she shared a moment with her mother.

Kit dropped the bottle and strode towards the lounge room. "Nan?" He got nothing in return.

He tried again "NAN!" still nothing, the lack of response set in a sense of panic that caused him to lose his footing and send him tumbling to the floor face first. He launched up, forging towards the lounge room where he could hear the faint sound of the pottery wheel. When he reached the room, he turned on the light and got a glimpse of something that forced him to turn it off again instantly. He stood there. He knew what he saw. Nan, slumped over her wheelchair. He dared not turn the light on again.

Josephine looked to her father. He lay there, useless, unfatherly.

She turned back to the screen. "Hey Mum."

Her mother smiled. "Hey JoJo."

The way she said her name caused Josephine to lose her breath, she knew this wasn't real but it didn't make it feel any less real.

"What are you doing?"

Her mother smiled again. "We're just in the park, are you going to come play with us?"

"Sure," Josephine responded. She couldn't help but be sucked in by the exchange, it was at once, tender and reminiscent and surreal. "Is Bevy there?"

"Yeah she's right here."

A girl who looked exactly like Josephine ran up with all the excitement of a four year old. "Hey, JoJo, you got my bracelet I made?"

Josephine nodded proudly. "I do." She lifted her wrist and revealed the exact same friendship bracelet.

Beverline beamed. "We can wear them together!"

Josephine wanted to cry. "Yeah, we can." She shifted back to bot control mode. "Put Mum back on."

Josephine's mother re-entered the frame. "Hey JoJo, you didn't answer my question."

"What was that mum?"

She softly shook her head. "Are you coming with us?" The question was more than just an invitation to play, it felt like an invitation to give up, become like her father, lose herself in these memories forever and ignore anything real, anything that could hurt you.

A tear ran down Josephine's cheek. The overwhelming nature of the interaction was just too much. "Not today, Mum."

The response didn't bother her mother in the slightest. "Of course, you've got important things to do. You go be that difference, little lady."

Josephine started crying. "I love you Mum."

Her mother didn't waver. The bot was only programmed to feedback positive responses. "I love you too sweetie."

Josephine turned back to her father, who had been watching and had somewhat sobered up. "Goodbye Mum."

Kit left the lights off and, step by step, made his way to his dead grandmother. Her back was facing him, her head slumped to the side, her wheelchair positioned facing the windows, her view, the stacked grid of apartment balconies. Kit stood over her. Slowly a high pitched sob squeezed out of his nose and mouth before it overtook his entire body and dropped him to his knees, where he finally turned to face her. "Nan," his voice high and wavering through the tears. Her eyes were open but they betrayed any sign of life. Her skin was blue and cold. Kit kept calling her name in the hope that she might wake up. "Nan, Nan, wake up, please, Nan wake up!" His cries grew louder with every request, his all out wail now echoed through the tiny apartment making it feel lonelier than ever.

Josephine threw up her OurCloud and commandeered the control panel of the screen being projected on the lounge room wall. Logging onto her father's profile, she started locating all the memory bot files. They loaded up in a constantly updating list. She was taken aback at how many files there were. The loading wheel seemed to never stop spinning. She looked back at her half-drunk father who was beginning to sober up from the shame of his addiction to the past.

Josephine turned back to the screen and saw the files were being categorized into headings. One for her twin sister Beverline and the other for her mother Hazeldine. Josephine paused for a moment, her entire past listed in moments, all of them memories extracted from her father's recollection.

Closing her eyes, she said the words, "Select all."

Montgomery clued onto what was happening and tried to stand up, but the alcohol in his system made it impossible.

Josephine kept her eyes closed. "Delete all files."

Montgomery kept scrambling. "Josephine no."

A prompt flicked up. "Are you sure you want to delete all files?"

Josephine nodded her head as her father finally got to his feet and lunged at her. "No!"

But it was too late. Josephine's OurCloud begun churning through each file one by one, wiping them off her father's home hard drive for good. Montgomery lost his balance and stumbled past his daughter and crashed into the table, his inebriated senses too woozy to control his body. In a desperate attempt, he commanded his own recovery of the files but was only presented with empty folder after empty folder. Staggering to his feet, he lurched over to Josephine who had primed herself. She was ready for anything.

He grabbed her arms and shook her. "What did you do? What did you do?" Tears streamed down his face, his voice cracked and high pitched.

Josephine stood there, her broken father had now caused her to cry.

"Why did you do that?" he screamed in her face.

She blasted back at him. "I had to. There was nothing left. You lost them. It's over. When are you going to wake up. It's time to start again!"

"Start what." Montgomery shouted back, his voice projecting all the loss from his past.

"Your life."

"I can't."

"You have to."

"I can't." He said it as if holding back some information.

"Why not?" She'd had enough and wanted an answer now.

"BECAUSE I KILLED THEM!!"

His answer created a vacuum in the room. For a second, the world had fallen silent as if everyone on the planet had heard his confession. Josephine couldn't move, the four words repeated in her head over and over again. The man in front of her was no longer her father but instead now the epicenter at which their family had imploded. Montgomery looked depleted, crushed, yet bizarrely relaxed, as if voicing that secret had released twenty years of guilt and pain.

He took a few steps back, making some space for Josephine who was still struggling to process the implications of what she just heard. "I killed them, Josephine."

Josephine wasn't present, she couldn't make eye contact, her face vacant, flushed of any emotion or life. "They didn't die in a car accident?"

He shook his head. "No. Your sister had Nox Anima. I tried to save her. It failed. Your mother killed herself not long after."

Josephine's legs gave out and she fell backwards breaking her fall with the couch. She held her head, her whole world was crashing down around her. "So why did you operate on Kit? Why did you say it worked?"

Montgomery breathed in deep. He looked at his daughter, her face stared back at him. The flash of her as a little girl blinked in front of his eyes and it made him smile, because he realized, after all these years, that his idea of success and failure had been all wrong. He had got it backwards. he answered Josephine, pride now in his voice, pride in the daughter he had raised. "Because the cure did work once. It worked with you."

Josephine went to talk but no words came out. Instead she choked on her lack of breath and felt light headed. She gripped the wall. The whole revelation was too much. Josephine grappled with the concept that she was once a Rat.

Montgomery lowered himself to the ground and sat there. The two of them said nothing. He was finally unburdening himself of this secret whilst simultaneously handballing it to Josephine to reconcile with—neither knew what to say or do, all that was apparent was that this had changed everything.

Kit's apartment was being dismantled like a Lego set; all of Kit's work mates criss-crossed pulling out fixtures, emptying bins, boxing goods. Kit stood there directing people whilst also collecting any items himself.

A familiar voice broke his flow. "So where do you need me?"

Jim stood, a tired smile over his face. Kit tried his best to suppress his own smile but he couldn't. At this point in his life, with Nan gone and Nox Anima now flowing through his veins, it meant the world to him to have his best friend back.

The damn wall broke and Kit finally smiled. "In the bathroom."

Jim walked past him and gave him his trademark comforting squeeze on his shoulder. Kit bathed in the warm feeling of Jim's presence before it was interrupted by a random removalist.

"Where do you want this?" He was holding one half of the pottery wheel.

Kit stared at it long and hard. "Just get it out of here." He watched the guy carry it away. His time was coming to an end. He was the last of his family, and making more clay pots wasn't going to change that.

Back in Montgomery's office, Josephine walked around. The room felt bigger now that it had been completely cleared. All that was left was a desk, a chair and a couple of white boards. It resembled a college class after the kids had vacated. It possessed that same haunting abandoned feeling. One thing had remained though. In the center of the room, lying in pain, was the Nox Anima console, looking as if someone had kicked it down.

Josephine walked over to it. It looked up at her, the weird dials and keys making that weird face, pleading her to hoist him back up, as if to say *I still hold so much hope, give me one more chance.*

She was about to bend down when the door creaked open and in walked Montgomery. He stopped, surprised to see her—maybe he was going to take a moment in this room, too. He hugged the walls as he walked around. They kept their distance from each other. The silence between them was long, neither knew how to instigate conversation, neither really knew what their place in the world was now. One had revealed his biggest failure, the other had snatched life from the jaws of death. The silence continued and went from awkward, to strange, to bearable and finally acceptable.

"I don't know why I pushed Nox Anima to be your life's work too. I guess I was just projecting my failures, figured you could make right what I got wrong."

Josephine kept her eyes on the ground.

"I'm sorry, it was never your battle, Josephine."

The apology forced Josephine to look up and look her dad in the eyes. The pause between them was intense.

"Maybe we don't get a choice of the battles we're given, only if we want to fight them," he added.

Josephine let out the biggest of sighs. "I think I'm done fighting, Dad." She leaned over the Nox Anima console. She studied its face.

Her father looked over and couldn't help the moment she was having with it.

Without looking back at him, she asked, "What else can this machine do?"

Kit walked around his now empty apartment. The removalists were gone, the doors and windows were now open and the blinds pulled back in a bid to freshen the place up. He walked from room to room, each one now just a hollow box waiting to be imbued with new furniture, photos, clothes and memories. Kit eventually made his way to the lounge room where he found Jim sitting down against the wall nursing a beer. Kit winced as he lowered himself down and slid against the wall next to his friend. He moved slowly into a comfortable position. Nox Anima was making everyday movements an effort now.

Jim reached underneath himself and pulled out an

envelope. It had Kit's name scribbled on the front, he handed it over. "I found this."

Kit looked it over, he recognized the handwriting. "Where?"

Jim shrugged and took a swig of his beer. "In the bathroom." He handed Kit the beer.

Kit took a swig before letting out the most tired of sighs. It was one of the few things that gave him relief. It was a pressure release, but mostly likely psychosomatic.

"So this is how it ends, huh?" Jim asked but he already knew the answer.

"I guess," Kit lamented, the reality was impossible to escape now.

This empty apartment staring back at them. All the items off to be pawned. The final step in a Rat's life, that was to liquidate your possessions and blow the money in a final explosion of life's vices.

"I'm sorta glad you're not doing the D Day party," Jim confessed. "I'm done celebrating death. I'm done being okay with it."

"Yeah, I don't think I can handle another one either, I'm not twenty anymore." Kit smirked as he reminisced. "I'm sorry I wasn't there for you and Tai, I fucked up."

Jim nodded. "Not your finest moment."

"So what are you going to do now?" Kit asked.

Jim weighed up his options. "I don't know, maybe take up pottery. I saw a wheel out there."

Kit nudged him in the ribs. "We had a good run, didn't we?"

That overall feeling of reminiscing came over Jim and made him smile. It felt warm, cozy and familiar. "The best," he responded, proud of the amount of life they crammed into their twenty seven years. Jim handed over the beer to Kit and hoisted himself up using Kit as his support. "I guess that's all that matters right? How we lived it." Jim walked off and left Kit there. "I'll see you around." Jim disappeared out the door.

The afternoon sounds of the Flats filtered into Kit's apartment. He was on the home stretch. He pulled out the envelope and felt the weight of it in his hands. Carefully he peeled the back of it and looked inside, finding an A4 piece of lined paper folded in half. Digging deeper, he pulled out a stack of 100 dollar bills.

Elizabeth picked at the ivy that covered the giant granite pillars of the university campus' law building. Josephine was with her and the lack of words between the two made it clear that a lot had already been said.

"I can't believe you're leaving me, what am I going to do? You're like my main girl."

Josephine shrugged. "You'll figure it out."

"What about the kids at the center?"

"I don't know, you talk to them, you like talking."

Elizabeth thought it over. "And what if I screw it up?"

Josephine chuckled and recalled something Kit said to her on her first date. "You've got eighty years to get it right."

The profoundness of the response wasn't lost on Elizabeth. The two of them smiled at each other. Josephine reached out her arms, ready to instigate a hug. Elizabeth walked into it and the two embraced in that style of hug that had a finality to it.

Elizabeth pulled back taking in her friend one last time. "I'm proud of you."

Josephine blushed before turning around and fading into the mass of students occupying the campus grounds. Elizabeth tried her best not to cry and let it all out in the biggest of exhales.

Josephine lay on a medical gurney. It looked familiar. Her gaze was unwavering, unblinking, as if she was priming herself for battle. In the background, her father moved around, the Nox Anima machine once again in front of him. Its sequence of buzzes and beeps and whirs calculated Josephine's vital signs before providing a read out on the glitchy touch screen, a remnant of damage done by Montgomery's kick to its head.

Back at the Flats, Kit emerged from the bottom of the towers with a duffle bag slung over his shoulder. He did a spin taking in his home for the past twenty seven years before turning back to find Jim waiting by his truck, smoking. Kit tossed his bag into the trailer and slingshot himself into the passenger seat. Jim threw away his cigarette and got inside himself before kicking the Liberace road monster into gear and tearing away. Kit looked out the window—his people, their lives, their stories, their struggles passing him by. It didn't really matter anymore, he had had his time. It was time to let someone else born with Nox Anima experience Rat life.

Montgomery placed the blue cap on Josephine's head. Purposefully, he attached each wire one by one. Josephine blinked every time each connection made that clacking sound. Each sound taking her deeper and deeper down a path. After attaching the last wire, Montgomery leaned over the machine and grabbed his daughter's hand. They stared at each other.

Nothing needed to be said but Montgomery was going to ask her again anyway, "Are you sure?"

Josephine nodded.

He leaned back and started tapping away at both the keypad and the screen. A large flashing prompt pulsed on and off: *Commence?* Montgomery hovered his fingers over the command. Josephine closed her eyes. He pressed the button, and the machine kicked into action, again producing the familiar calculating sequence of beeps and whirs.

Montgomery stood up and walked out of the room. The console's fans began to kick in, cooling the system, the machine working in overdrive as it powered through its computations. The electrodes and wires orchestrated all types of colors, but Josephine was none the wiser. The anesthetic had taken hold and she had fallen asleep.

Jim pulled up to the airport. Planes roared overhead, people arrived and exited in haste so as not to miss their flights. Jim hung around doing a sterling job of keeping in his emotions whilst Kit grabbed his bag from the trailer.

Kit turned to him and tilted his head.

Jim opened his arms and the two buddies hugged. Both rested their heads on each other's shoulders and kept their eyes open. The moment was real, two plus decades of friendship was coming to a physical end.

Jim pulled away and looked at him. "Find the gems, mutherfucker, find the gems."

Kit winked and walked away. Jim swallowed the cryball stuck in his throat and got back into his truck.

In the airport Kit walked up to the ticket board. The sign flickered over giving a refresh of all the departures and arrivals. Kit's flight buzzed on screen with the words *Flight delayed*. A collective groan was heard from a bunch of the soon to be passengers. It didn't bother Kit. Finally, for the first time in his life, he wasn't in a rush.

Josephine's eyes snapped open. She gulped in a few deep breaths and sat up. It was a mirror image of when Kit had done the same months ago. She looked around and the room was empty—just the giant open curtains letting in the light that reflected off the greenery outside. Taking off the helmet, she leaped off the bed and attempted to run for the door. Her legs gave way and she staggered in a diagonal line before hitting the ground. She hoisted herself up with her palms and forced herself back onto her feet. Stepping forward again, she made sure her footing was true and headed for the door.

Jim parked his truck underneath the towers. The last few days had been heavy. He never thought he'd be the last one standing, but that was usually the case. It was always the one you least expected that made it the farthest. He trudged his way up the stairs to his apartment. He cast his eyes down, the weight of now being alone was starting to dawn on him. Like those who retired early where the lack of mental stimulation caused their brains to atrophy, those who were the last ones left usually activated Nox Anima purely from the grief and the loneliness.

Jim pulled out his keys ready to enter his apartment when something sitting on the stairs stopped him.

It was Josephine and her look said it all. "We need to talk."

Back at the airport, Kit stretched over a row of uncomfortable faux leather seats. His oversized headphones sat on his ears as he listened to *93 til infinity* by Souls of Mischief. He focused his attention on the glass ceiling. Clouds slowly floated by while randomly intercut by propulsive jets powering through them. He wasn't thinking of anything—in fact he was too exhausted and too deep into his mutation to really use his brain. It was a relief.

Jim was back at the wheel of his truck as he pushed the shiny gold and silver beast to its limits through downtown traffic. Josephine gripped the handle with her hand and steadied herself on the dashboard with her other.

Jim yanked the wheel and fishtailed the entire truck around the corner of an intersection before slamming the horn with his fist. "Come on! Out of the way!" He looked back at the driver. "God damn idiot." He chuckled and looked over to Josephine. "You doing okay?"

She nodded in compliance but she was far from calm.

Kit was now asleep. A boarding call came over the PA system. People around him rose off their chairs and hoisted their bags on their shoulders. Kit remained asleep. A soft hand gently shook his foot which in turn caused him to gently wake up. Gingerly, he sat up and slid off his headphones.

A calm voice queried him, "Are you on this flight, sir?"

Kit smiled and nodded before swinging his legs over and rubbing the sleep from his eyes. He stood up, stretched, and looked around—again just a bunch of strangers, mostly older Rats spending their cash on life experiences before they died. Grabbing his bag, he ambled towards the row of people lined up behind the ticket scanner.

Jim's truck came to a mangled stop right at the same spot he had dropped off Kit. Josephine launched out of the truck whilst Jim leaned out the window and yelled "Go! Go! Go!"

She bombed for the entrance doing her best to dodge and weave the suitcases and oblivious travelers attempting to get their shit together. Josephine sprinted through the entrance but had no idea where she was going. Darting between the criss-cross of luggage being wheeled around her, she spotted the departures board.

Scanning it, she couldn't see his flight. She calmed herself down and scanned it again. There it was: Tropea, boarding now!

Kit stood in line but something compelled him to pull away. He stepped back and let those behind him go through first. Looking around, he hoped that someone would chase after him, that someone would still want him in their life… that Josephine would be here with him.

Josephine pumped her legs and arms as she counted each gate in passing. Still she saw no sign of him.

Eventually the second last passenger scanned their ticket. Kit remained but he knew it was time to face facts. He was doing this alone.

The attendant smiled at him. "Sir, you boarding this flight?"

Kit nodded, his whole body admitting defeat. Reluctantly, he scanned his ticket and walked through. His figure slunked down the ramp as the attendants packed up their counters and closed the doors.

Josephine arrived moments later, frantically looking around. She was looking the wrong way, before finally turning to spot Kit's gate. It was bare, the doors were closed, no sign of attendants or passengers. She raced to the doors and tried to open them but they were sealed shut. She paced around rubbing her temples. She couldn't fathom the idea that this was how it was going to end.

Kit made his way to his seat. After stuffing his bag overhead, he shuffled himself to the window seat and looked out to the giant glass façade of the airport. He could feel the tears building behind his eyes so he turned to the window to hide himself, but caught his grief in the reflection of the glass.

Josephine sat at the gate looking out from the other side of the giant glass window. She was crying, too, but didn't care if anyone saw her. She wondered if he felt the same, if only she knew that he did.

CHAPTER 29
WHAT WOULD YOU DO
WITH THAT TIME?

Nan's voice rang through Kit's head. "Every day. Just after you'd left for work and just before you came home. I found myself sitting by my wheel staring into the towers."

A low hanging sun danced off turquoise waters only found in the Mediterranean. The sea was bluer than the sky. A distant hum of activity could be heard—music, bars, laughter, chatter, mopeds.

Nan's voice continued. "These spiritless buildings that we came to call home were actually alive. Not with people but with stories."

A giant splash broke the surface of the sea and out rocketed Kit from underneath. He settled into a float, covered in a thin film of crystal salt water. "This is your story, Kit. Even if there is no one to hear it. You must make it one worth telling."

The water beaded over his Nox Anima Cross. The cross was now a deep red. His face was now gaunt, his body lacking that sturdiness, the muscle now wasting away, but it was offset by the tan he had acquired and the hair and stubble he had grown. He floated for a moment. His eyes sparkling from the reflection of the sea, but even the beauty of the surroundings couldn't hide the sorrow behind his eyes.

A fourteen-year-old local boy drove Kit around the winding roads on a scooter. Mile high vegetation lined both sides, while the breeze hit his face, hair and chest. He closed his eyes and let it wrap around him. The experience was the same as the one he gave Josephine on his bike on their first date, and he raised his arms out just like she did. "I've played my part. Now it's time for you to find the ending that best fits your story."

The scooter passed a sign that read: *TROPEA Pop 6,462 (Nox Anima Sufferers Welcome)*.

In his hotel room, Kit sat on his bed reading the letter. It was the envelope that Jim had found in his house during the clean out. It was Nan's final words. Her voice continued in his head, "If you're reading this letter I want you to know I held on as long as I could. But as you understand, it's not always our choice when we're lifted from this earth. I heard a saying once, when you and I were going for one of our walks. It was spoken by your friend Tai, maybe that's why I remembered it. She simply said: "Find the Gems.""

Kit folded the letter and rested his head back on the cushion, and the sun from the window of the room hit his face. Reaching over to the bedside table, he grabbed something and studied it. It was the photo of his parents when they were here years ago.

That night Kit wandered the streets of the beach town. It was ancient, built in a time when things were simple—you lived, you worked, you died. Kit wore a pair of shorts and a loose fitting shirt. If it wasn't for his fading body he really had adapted to the speed of beach life. He navigated the town's population which had exploded over the years as it had become a safe haven for Rats enjoying their last days. The balmy air and tanned skin on show made the holidayers forget why they were really there. Kit ignored all of it, like he was looking for something. He craned his neck left and right until he stopped mid stride at the sight of a bar.

Kit carefully crept inside. The idea of tracing the steps his parents had trodden made him nervous but also humbled him and connected him to them once more. Every step in this bar was precious, he wanted to savor it. Every texture a possible connection to the past. It was a quaint establishment that wasn't overly reliant on tourists.

Kit grabbed the photo of his mum and dad and lifted it. The photo matched perfectly, the 1000 year old white sandstone brick arch that stood behind his parents remained untouched in front of him right at that moment.

Over in the corner, Kit spotted a wall. It was plastered with photos, so many that they had raised the level of the wall a couple of inches. Kit moved over and ran his eyes over them, a collection of people, couples, families, happy moments but most of all, final moments. Kit grabbed one of the pins and stuck the photo of his parents right in the center. He admired it and sat in that moment. He felt closer to them than he had ever felt.

As he turned to leave, something in his peripheral vision pulled him back. He turned around to face the wall of photos and froze. There, a few inches away from the photo of his parents was a photo of himself and Josephine. The photo the two of them took on her bed when he had an OurCloud. He looked around expecting everyone to be experiencing the same rush of emotions he was but everybody in the bar went about their business. He went to touch it. The photo was real and this wasn't a joke. He blazed out of the bar, his actions causing everyone to stop their meals and watch him.

Outside Kit tumbled his way through the holiday-makers. His feet and head couldn't break the crowd quick enough. He reached the middle of the piazza and subsequently a gridlock made of a congregating crowd. Lurching his neck and peering over, he realized everyone had formed around a street performer. He tried to shuffle left and right but it was no use. He was boxed in. Suddenly the crowd erupted into clapping and cheers. The crowd finally dispersed giving Kit a chance to sneak looks through the widening gaps. As the performers collected their things, Kit spotted a face on the other side of the crowd.

It was Josephine. She looked incredible. She was wearing a blue and yellow sundress and gold sandals; her hair was loose. She looked like a different person, like a weight had been lifted off of her, but she hadn't noticed Kit yet. Kit pushed his way around the remaining folks before finally Josephine turned and locked onto him. The sight of each other forced them into a state of shock. They didn't run for each other right away. This was the most important moment in their lives and they knew it. Finally, Kit had had enough. He pushed his way through instigating the same from Josephine.

The two of them bullocked through the loitering people until the space between them finally shrunk and they collided into each other. Kit caught Josephine in his arms and they leaned back their heads to get a look at each other up close. He didn't want to stop staring at her, the pure joy radiating from his eyes and smile gave him an almost out of body experience. A feeling of wholeness so consuming his body could not contain it. He ran his hand over her shoulder and noticed a blue light reflecting onto his fingers. He looked back to her in disbelief. She offered him that unwavering stare—the one she had used so many times before to excite crowds at her rallies.

Josephine was part of his world now. She had given herself Nox Anima.

They kissed, and the crowds walked around them. In a world desperate to keep them apart, these two found each other. It was no longer about the time they had lost, or the time they had left but the moments they had already lived.

EPILOGUE

Three weeks later, Kit died. Josephine took him to the highest lookout she could find in the town and together, the two of them, amongst crumbling historic sandstone, watched the sunset for the last time. The town offered a burial service, and she finally put Kit to rest the next day. She didn't want to spend any more time in the town. The time she spent there with Kit was enough. At twenty-three, and most likely the only person to give herself Nox Anima, or at least re activate it, she had no idea how many years she had left. And neither did her father. Maybe her cross would appear tomorrow, or next year, or never. Or maybe the machine was as ineffective at re activating Nox Anima as it was curing it.

On the plane ride home, Josephine looked out the window. Something about being 30,000 feet high made her feel more emotional. She didn't watch any movies or eat for the entire flight. She just sat there, looking at the clouds, falling asleep, then waking up and doing it all over again. She didn't want to cloud the emotion she was feeling with in-flight entertainment. She was sad, sadder than she had ever been in her life and she wanted to feel all of it. It was the first time she had felt this way and it signaled to her that it was worth it, that he was worth it.

When she arrived home, she found her father had sold his house and moved into a modest apartment in the city. He'd started exercising and had taken up guest lecturing at her old university. His course was Nox Anima and its effects on modern technology and medicine. Montgomery knew his time was almost up, but hoped that maybe he would spark the mind who could finish what he started.

Josephine decided that her decision to quit her life's ambition was a tad too hasty, but also came to recognize that Kit was probably right, too, that trying to do the work she did as a Clean Skin was only going to get her so far. She didn't want to embark on any career or profession that would rob her of her focus, so she took a job at a café, something where she could punch in and out.

So with her new found "Ratness," she embarked on her rallies and mentoring again, but this time hosting them on the other side of town but also on campuses around the state. It didn't take long for them to pick up more momentum and critical mass than she had ever imagined. Now that she was one of them, a sense of freedom had come over her. She had nothing to lose. In their eyes, this woman was the real deal; a genuine Rat and they fed off that. That old Josephine—the one who had cloistered herself within the bubble of university life—was unrecognizable now. There was a toughness to her, a don't give damn energy, she would have eaten the old Josephine for breakfast.

Eventually her profile and her movement for equal rights had grown so big that the inevitable question about her past surfaced. People wanted to know how this young woman, seemingly from nowhere, became the most prominent voice for those with Nox Anima in the country. Josephine told them the truth, or a version of the truth, that she had always had Nox Anima, that the shame of society had forced her to hide it and now it was her duty to break that stigma of the mutation and make it commonplace amongst everyone.

Before her thirtieth birthday and still showing no sign of Nox Anima, and with seven years of rallies, protests, appeals to the courts and endless meetings with lawmakers, Josephine had her first win, a big win. She and the greater public had convinced the government to hold a referendum on Nox Anima voting rights. The legislation, if passed, would allow those with Nox Anima to vote in the next upcoming election. Not only that, it would allow those with Nox Anima to run for local and state office, not just as an outlier tokenistic candidate, but as a real candidate attached to a real political party. They could pass through bills that would allow sufferers to apply for higher education and even engage in relationships with non-sufferers.

A week later the legislation passed. It was named the K.I.T Law. It stood for Kind, Inclusive and Tolerant, and Josephine, for the first time in seven years, took a breath. She looked back on Kit and the impact he had had on her life. She had been in relationships since his passing—some were good, others were okay, and a few were downright average, but none of them inspired her or challenged her and none were as empowering as her time with Kit.

She was now thirty and she didn't know what was going to happen next. If a cross was to appear on her shoulder tomorrow she was okay with that. But if by chance there was still another seventy years to live she was okay with that too, because now she knew, she had seventy years to get it right.